Maid Mary Anne

**Other books by
Ann M. Martin**

Rachel Parker, Kindergarten Show-off

Eleven Kids, One Summer

Ma and Pa Dracula

Yours Turly, Shirley

Ten Kids, No Pets

Slam Book

Just a Summer Romance

Missing Since Monday

With You and Without You

Me and Katie (the Pest)

Stage Fright

Inside Out

Bummer Summer

Maid Mary Anne
Ann M. Martin

AN
APPLE
PAPERBACK

SCHOLASTIC INC.
New York Toronto London Auckland Sydney

ISBN 0-590-47004-3

12 11 10 9 8 7 6 5 4 3 2 1   3 4 5 6 7 8/9

Printed in the U.S.A.   40

First Scholastic printing, August 1993

*The author gratefully acknowledges
Nola Thacker
for her help in
preparing this manuscript.*

Maid Mary Anne

CHAPTER 1

"Happy families are all alike." That's a quote, sort of, in case you wondered, from a book called *Anna Karenina* by a Russian writer named Leo Tolstoy. It's the very first line of the book, which has about a million more lines — it's a long book.

Have I read it? Don't worry. I haven't. At least not yet. But as a member of the Baby-sitters Club (more about that later), I've had the chance to meet someone who has. Our Baby-sitters Club vice-president Claudia Kishi's older sister, Janine, who is a genuine genius, has read the whole book. Once when I was at Claudia's I told Janine about a home-work assignment: to write a memorable, un-forgettable opening sentence for a story. That's when she told me the quote.

I was thinking about that quote on a warm, sunny summer Saturday while I was eating breakfast with my family. My stepsister Dawn

Schafer was polishing off a bowl of granola with plain yogurt and fruit. My father was carefully cutting a second bagel in half, and spreading it with *precisely* one tablespoon of cream cheese. My stepmother Sharon was frowning down at her place as if she had mislaid something (she's a little, well, disorganized). I was eating a toasted bagel with lots and lots of butter and raspberry jam.

I stopped to look around the table and thought about what Tolstoy had said, and wondered if it were true. I knew we were a happy family, but I was pretty sure we weren't like any other families I knew.

For example, Dawn was my best friend before she was my stepsister. And I have a stepbrother, Jeff, who is Dawn's younger brother, but who lives in California with his and Dawn's father. And Sharon and my father used to date (years and *years* ago) right here in Stoneybrook where we live. And . . .

Wait. I better begin at the beginning.

I'm Mary Anne Spier. I'm thirteen years old and I'm in the eighth grade at Stoneybrook Middle School. I'm the secretary of the Babysitters Club (my friends and I call it the BSC) and I live in a spooky old farmhouse with my father and my stepmother and Dawn. Dawn is also in the eighth grade at SMS and a member of the BSC.

But it wasn't always that way. I was an only child. My mother died when I was just a baby, and my father raised me on his own. Meanwhile, Dawn's parents got divorced and Dawn's mother decided to move back to Stoneybrook, because it was her hometown. She brought Dawn and Jeff with her.

Dawn and I became friends and she joined the Baby-sitters Club (she's the alternate officer). And *then* we discovered that her mother and my father used to know each other when they were in high school and living in Stoneybrook.

How did Dawn and I turn out to be such great detectives? Well, we found my dad's and Dawn's mother's high school yearbooks. Inside were these really sweet love notes they'd written to each other at the end of their senior year. That's when Dawn and I realized that not only had her mother and my father known each other, they'd been in love!

Pretty romantic. It was more romantic when (with a little help from Dawn and me), Dad and Sharon began to date again. And even though they are very different people, they fell in love and got married. So Dad and I (and my gray kitten Tigger) moved out of our house and into Dawn's house and now we are one big (well, bigger than just my dad and me) happy family.

But happy families can't all be alike, I don't know any family that is just like mine. Not only are we completely different from other families, but the members of my famly are pretty different from each other.

For example, my father is a very organized, meticulous person. He always buttons his coats and sweaters and shirts the same way, from bottom to top, because that way he won't waste any time making a mistake and having the buttons come out uneven so he has to do it all over again. He alphabetizes things, like the stuff in the bathroom cabinet. And he used the same strict, by-the-book method to raise me. Don't misunderstand me. I love my father very much. He's a warm and caring person. But since he had to be both my mother *and* my father, he was very careful. Until not long ago, I used to have to wear my hair in braids and dress in conservative, little-girl clothes. And when most of my friends got their ears pierced, I wasn't allowed to. Gradually I managed to convince him to be a little less strict (to let me wear my hair loose and get some more stylish clothes), but marriage to Sharon was what really loosened him up. (Now I can even wear a little makeup, but still no pierced ears. Yet!)

Sharon's personality couldn't be more different than my father's. She might not notice if her sweater or coat were buttoned up the wrong way — or maybe even if it were inside out or backwards. If she were going to organize the bathroom cabinet, she'd probably arrange things according to color, or shape. And it's a definite possibility that sooner or later you'd look in the cabinet and find something that didn't belong at all, like a letter stamped and ready to be mailed. Sharon is absentminded that way. But she's a wonderful person, and she and my father are really happy together.

Dawn and I are pretty opposite, too. For instance, our looks. I'm monochromatic, with brown hair and brown eyes. Dawn has incredible long, pale, pale blonde hair and blue eyes. Also, she will eat only healthy food: tofu, granola, yogurt, sprouts, hardly any sweets, and *no* red meat. She loves to read ghost stories. And she's a real individualist: she has two holes pierced in each ear. She dresses in whatever way she feels like dressing, and doesn't worry about wearing what everybody else is wearing. And although Dawn is very perceptive and kindhearted and even-tempered, she's not afraid to take a stand on what she believes in, like protecting the environment.

That's one of the things I admire most about Dawn, and one of the ways in which we are really different. I'm very shy and I hate confrontations. I guess that's because I'm sensitive. I cry easily over stuff that sometimes takes even *me* by surprise — not just the sad things, but things such as movies that have happy endings.

And I still dress sort of conservatively (although not like a little kid anymore). I don't mind the winters here, either, although Dawn does. She even thinks our summers don't quite measure up to California weather standards.

Dawn misses California and her father and Jeff sometimes. (Back before my dad and Sharon even planned to get married, Jeff decided he would be happier living in California with his dad.) It was really hard for Dawn to decide where to live when her little brother wanted to go back. But at last Dawn stayed here in Stoneybrook.

I'm super glad she did.

Because as different as we all are (and as different as we are from other families) I love being a part of our family. It's corny, maybe, but it's true.

So that's what I was thinking, looking dreamily around the kitchen. What a nice, happy, unlike-other-families family.

Then I saw the kitchen clock.

I blinked. I couldn't believe how late it was.

I jumped up and grabbed my plate.

"Mary Anne?" said my father, looking startled.

"I'm sitting for the Arnold twins this morning. I better get ready," I explained.

"If you'll put your plate in the sink, I'll wash it," said Dawn.

I threw her a grateful smile. "Thanks."

As I left the table, Sharon looked up and the worried frown left her face. "Plate! Now I remember!" she cried. "The laundry soap! I put it in the kitchen cabinet with the dishes!"

I heard Sharon and my father and Dawn start to laugh as I hurried to my room to get ready for my baby-sitting job.

It was nice of Dawn to volunteer to take my dishwashing chores for that morning, I thought, as I hustled around getting ready. It wasn't a big deal, but it was thoughtful.

Would I have thought to do that?

Of course I would, I told myself, but I wasn't so sure. I'd been feeling just the opposite of thoughtful and considerate lately. Sort of, well, too self-involved. Maybe even self-centered. Hateful words to think about anybody, but especially about myself.

It had started just before school ended on Friday with something Dawn had said. I'd been worrying and worrying about a speech I had to give for English and when I asked

Dawn, for about the thousandth time, what she thought people would think, she'd said, trying to be helpful, "Hey, Mary Anne, don't worry. They're not thinking only of you. Everyone's got all kinds of things going on in their lives. If you think of something besides yourself, it'll make it a lot easier."

Was I too self-centered? Too self-involved?

I had decided that I wasn't going to let that happen. From now on, I was going to try to put others first, and me and my needs (and selfish worries) second.

In spite of all this thinking I was doing, I got ready in record time. In fact, Dawn and my father were still sitting at the table when I hurried back downstairs. Sharon was just pushing one of the kitchen windows open.

"It's a beautiful day," she said. "Plenty of sun!"

"It sure is," I said. "Can I do anything while I'm out? Any errands?"

Looking faintly mystified, Sharon and my father shook their heads.

"Dawn?" I asked.

"No, thanks, Mary Anne," Dawn turned her face to the window. "The sun feels good. It makes me miss Jeff and California and . . ." her voice trailed off.

"Well," I said cheerfully, "I just hope I can

persuade the Arnolds to do something out-doors. It's way too nice to stay inside. 'Bye!"

I waved to everybody and hustled out the door. I was just going to make it on time.

Mrs. Arnold met me at the door and left her house almost as quickly as I'd left mine, waving good-bye to Marilyn and Carolyn in a jingle of bracelets and necklaces, promising she'd be back from her meeting by two o'clock.

I left the door open after Mrs. Arnold had driven away and motioned to the world outside. "Why don't we go exploring?" I asked the twins.

The idea appealed to Carolyn instantly. She wants to be a scientist and once even "invented" a very real-looking time machine in her basement. Although she and Marilyn are twins, and look exactly alike (except that Carolyn has shorter hair and a tiny mole under her left eye, and Marilyn has a tiny mole under her right eye, like mirror images), they're as different as Dawn and I, in a way. Marilyn is not at all scientific. She's interested in music — in fact, she's taken piano lessons since she was four — and she's very strict about practicing the piano at least half an hour every day. Meanwhile, Carolyn is tone-deaf.

"I'll get my notebook," Carolyn went on. "I can make observations about the trip."

"Good idea." As Carolyn hurried away I looked at Marilyn. "What about you, Marilyn? You want to go exploring?"

"I *think* so," answered Marilyn. "We're not going to get lost, though, are we?"

"No, we won't get lost," I promised, hiding a smile.

"Okay." She nodded. "Columbus got lost," she explained. "He *thought* he was on his way to India, but he was wrong."

"Nobody's perfect," I said. "But we're not going all the way to India. We're just going to walk along Burnt Hill Road. Maybe we can visit the Stones' farm. It's a little past my house."

"A farm!" said Carolyn, who had returned clutching an official-looking notebook and a pen. "Great!"

"Come on, then," I said, taking Marilyn and Carolyn each by the hand. "Maybe there'll even be a surprise when we get there."

I was thinking about Elvira Stone. She's not a member of the Stone family, exactly. What she is, is a goat. A very, very cute baby goat that Dawn and I goat-sat for this past spring.

While Carolyn and Marilyn tried to guess what the surprise might be, and I gave them mysterious hints, we walked slowly down Burnt Hill Road. In addition to asking me questions about the surprise, Carolyn had to stop every few minutes to flip her notebook open and write "observations" in it. But it was Marilyn who startled me when she tilted her head and said, "Listen."

We stopped and listened. I heard the sound of a lawn mower, the faint mooing of a cow, the wind in the trees, and the usual bird song noises.

"What is it?" I asked Marilyn.

"It's a cardinal," she said.

I listened. The usual bird song noises. All different kinds.

Then Marilyn said, "That . . ." and I heard (I think) the cardinal's song. I wouldn't have known it, or picked it out from the other bird sounds.

I was impressed.

"That's great, Marilyn," I told her.

Carolyn looked puzzled. "How can you tell which one it is?"

"It sounds different," explained Marilyn.

"It does? Hmmm." Carolyn listened for a moment, then flipped open her book and wrote something down.

We passed my house and soon came to the Stones' farm. As we were crossing the road, a quail burst out from the tall grass at the side of the road and raced across.

"A quail," said Carolyn, writing in her book. "Also known as the bobwhite for its song."

As if to help Carolyn out, we heard "bob-white, bobwhite, bobwhite"! We looked at each other. "Bobwhite!" cried Carolyn happily, and Marilyn nodded.

We passed the Stones' truly awesome vegetable garden, complete with a scarecrow.

"Wow," breathed Marilyn. "Is that the surprise. A *real* scarecrow?"

"No," I said.

We skirted a rusty tractor and were just walking toward the house when Mrs. Stone came out of the barn. Chickens scattered in front of her as she walked briskly forward.

I raised my hand and waved.

"Mary Anne!" she said.

"Hi, Mrs. Stone," I answered. "I've brought Marilyn and Carolyn Arnold to visit your farm — and to see Elvira."

"Welcome, Marilyn and Carolyn," Mrs. Stone said.

"Hello, Mrs. Stone," said Marilyn and Carolyn, at exactly the same time and in the same tone of voice. They didn't even seem to notice.

"Who's Elvira?" asked Marilyn.

"Is that the surprise?" asked Carolyn.

"You'll see," I told them.

Mrs. Stone dipped her hand in the bucket, scattering corn around her feet. There was a flurry of chickens, scratching and squawking.

Carolyn began making notes as fast as she could.

"Here," said Mrs. Stone. "Why don't you feed them some corn, too?"

So Marilyn and Carolyn each reached in the bucket and scattered handfuls of corn for the chickens. Mrs. Stone stepped to one side and we watched.

"They're so funny," said Carolyn, as she emptied the last of the corn out.

"Was that the surprise?" asked Marilyn.

"No," I said.

"Elvira?" said Mrs. Stone softly to me.

I nodded.

"Okay," said Mrs. Stone. "One surprise, coming up."

Well, Elvira, the cutest baby goat in the world, was of course a big hit. She bounded across the pen when she saw us and butted her head between the fence rails. "Beaaaah," she said.

The twins began to coo and pet her.

But I was almost as surprised as they were.

"Wow, she's really grown," I said to Mrs. Stone.

"Yes. But she's still a baby at heart," she replied fondly.

When we finally persuaded the twins to say good-bye to Elvira, Mrs. Stone gave us a tour of the rest of the farm. Carolyn's pen flew as she took notes. Marilyn even helped Carolyn, pointing out things that Carolyn might have missed, such as "That pig has nine babies, Carolyn. Did you write that down?"

Mrs. Stone smiled and turned to me. "It's true, isn't it, Mary Anne, that you like sewing and needlework?"

"Yes, it is," I said. "I'm just learning, though."

"Have you ever met Mrs. Towne? She lives just down the road." She waved in the direction in which we'd come. She's quite a seamstress — and a gardener. You might have noticed her garden before."

I thought I had. Not many houses are on our road.

"Mrs. Towne is an expert at smocking and quilting and French hand sewing. You should meet her, and see her work. She's won quite a few prizes for it. It's really wonderful."

"I'd like that," I told Mrs. Stone. "A lot!" (Even though I was a *disaster* in home ec, I still love sewing.)

Just then a goose came marching up to us, stretching its neck and honking.

"Uh-oh!" said Marilyn.

"Oh no!" said Carolyn.

"Don't worry," said Mrs. Stone. "That's

Screaming Yellow Honker. He's our watch goose."

I was as fascinated as Marilyn and Carolyn by the idea of a watch goose, and I listened intently as she told us about Honker. But I didn't forget about Mrs. Towne, and as we were walking home a little later, I made a point of looking for her house. Sure enough, there it was, halfway between the Stones' farm and our house, sitting back on about an acre of cleared land set in the woods by the road. Stone fences marked the edges of it, and lined the driveway. It was a tidy old white farmhouse, with all kinds of flowers and trees around it: azaleas, which were just finishing blooming, late daffodils, sweet alyssum with its honey smell, zinnias. I recognized beds of vegetables, too, tomatoes and foot-high stalks of sweet corn. If Mrs. Towne was as good at sewing as she was at gardening, I could learn plenty from her.

But how would I meet her? I couldn't just walk up to her door and knock. I wondered if she had any children, and might need a baby-sitter. That would be one way to meet her.

Then I remembered some of the things Mrs. Stone had said: that Mrs. Towne was a widow.

Making those tiny little perfect stitches required good eyesight and Mrs. Towne, at her age, had better eyesight than most people at any age. I decided Mrs. Towne might be older. So the baby-sitter idea was out. She probably didn't have children, or if she did, they were all grown up.

Her gardens, I thought suddenly, were as beautiful as a patchwork quilt against the grass. More than ever, I wanted to meet her. I wished I weren't so shy.

I sighed.

"Mary Anne?" asked Carolyn, and I realized I had stopped all together and was staring at the house.

"Oops. Sorry." I said. "We'd better get moving. Your mother will be home any minute and she'll wonder where you are."

Marilyn giggled. "We'll tell her we got lost exploring. We took a wrong turn and ended up in India and were eaten by tigers!"

"Or in the desert and were attacked by wild desert rattlesnakes!" said Carolyn.

"In the mountains and were chased by a bear!" answered Marilyn instantly.

They played the game all the way home. I laughed at the wild scenarios they concocted. But I have to admit, I concocted some almost as wild and just as unlikely myself — for meeting Mrs. Towne.

CHAPTER 2

"Order in the club!" said Jessi Ramsey, holding up a Cheez Doodle.

Kristy Thomas, who is the president of the Baby-sitters Club and a stickler for organization, looked at Jessi sternly. She pulled the green visor she always wears for meetings down over her eyes, straightened up in the director's chair (where she always sits), and said (as she always does), "This meeting of the Baby-sitters Club will come to order. Is there any new business?"

"Here's some new food," said a muffled voice from the closet. A moment later Claudia Kishi backed out, holding an unopened bag of plain pretzels in one hand, and an unopened bag of chocolate-dipped pretzels in another.

"Great," said Mallory Pike, pushing her glasses up her nose in a characteristic gesture. "I'm starving."

Claudia grinned and tossed the chocolate pretzels to Mallory, who was sitting on the floor, leaning against the bed. She handed the other bag to Stacey McGill, who was sitting next to her.

"Well?" said Kristy loudly.

"No new business, at least not for me," said Stacey, ripping open the bag, taking out some pretzels, and offering the bag to Dawn.

Kristy looked around the room. We shook our heads.

Then Stacey said, "Of course, it *is* dues day."

We groaned (which we always do) but we got out our money and handed it over to Stacey. She's our treasurer.

In case you hadn't guessed, I was at a meeting of the Baby-sitters Club.

What (or who) is the Baby-sitters Club?

Well, the BSC started as an idea in Kristy's organized brain. Kristy was listening to her mother try to find a baby-sitter one night, calling person after person with no success, and she thought, wouldn't it be great if someone could make just one phone call and reach several available baby-sitters?

With Kristy, the thought is almost always the parent to the action, meaning that within no time at all, she'd begun organizing a baby-sitting club. And the rest, as they say, is history.

Because it was a super idea.

But then Kristy's ideas usually are. She's one of the most organized people I know, and we've known each other and been best friends for as long as I can remember, even though we are *so* different. Kristy is outgoing, out-spoken, out-everything. She can be bossy and maddening, but those are the qualities that make her a great BSC president. I wouldn't be surprised if someday she becomes President of the United States.

Some examples of why she'd make a great President? Well, Kristy not only thought of the BSC, she also came up with the idea of keeping a BSC notebook. The notebook is like a diary for the members of the BSC. Each of us writes about our sitting jobs, describing what happened. Then the rest of us are responsible for reading the notebook once a week. We may not always like doing it, especially those of us who are not as organized as Kristy, but that notebook has been very, very useful.

Kristy also created the Kid-Kits. Kid-Kits are cardboard boxes filled with inexpensive toys, games, and books. A lot of it is old stuff we have around our houses, things we've out-grown. The rest we buy with some of our club dues. We don't take the Kid-Kits to every baby-sitting job, because then they'd lose their novelty appeal — but they're a big hit whenever we do. For the kids, it's like having a whole new box of toys to play with.

And then there's the record book, also Kristy's idea. The record book is the client list, with names, addresses, phone numbers, wages, plus the schedule of all our jobs. As secretary of the BSC, I'm in charge of keeping the record book straight.

Kristy also founded Kristy's Krushers, a softball team for all the kids we baby-sit for who aren't quite ready for Little League. The Krushers range from age two and a half to age eight, and although they may not always win their games when it comes to keeping score, they always win when it comes to having fun.

How do I know so much about Kristy? Well, she and I have known each other since we were babies. We're best friends, even though, as you can see, we're complete opposites.

Well, not *complete* opposites. Some things about us are sort of similar. We're both short, for example. And Kristy's mother got married again, just like my father did, so Kristy got a new family, too.

Kristy used to live in the house next door to where I used to live, and across the street from Claudia's. Her father left when her younger brother, David Michael, was a baby. Just walked out, never said he was sorry or even explained — at least not to Kristy. That left Mrs. Thomas to take care of four kids, Kristy, her two older brothers Charlie and Sam, and of course, David Michael. She did it, but I don't think it was easy. (Maybe that's where Kristy got her super-organizational skills from.) Then Mrs. Thomas fell in love, and it turned out that Watson Brewer, the man she fell in love with, was a millionaire. He and Kristy's mom got married and they all moved into his mansion.

And now the mansion is filling up! Watson has two kids from his first marriage, who live in the Brewers' house on alternate weekends and holidays, plus Emily Michelle, an adopted Vietnamese girl. Also, Kristy's grandmother, Nannie, lives with them and helps keep an eye on all the kids and what seems like dozens of pets.

So it's a good thing Kristy doesn't mind making herself heard. In the Brewer household, you really do have to speak up!

Anyway, that's how the BSC got started. Kristy, Claudia, and I were charter members. But because it was such a great idea, in no time at all, the BSC needed more members, which is how Stacey joined us.

Stacey's parents moved to Stoneybrook when her father's office transferred him here. Then her parents got divorced and Mr. McGill moved back to New York, while Stacey's mom stayed in Stoneybrook. Stacey had a hard time trying to decide whether to go back to New York with her father, or stay here in "the country" with her mom.

Because for Stacey, the tree-lined streets and quiet sidewalks of Stoneybrook really are the country. Stacey is a true New Yorker: she loves bright lights, crowds of people, can sleep through any amount of noise, and is completely unflappable. The last quality, as you might imagine, is an excellent one for a successful baby-sitter.

It's also a good quality for Stacey because she is diabetic. That means her body can't handle the sugar in her blood and she could get very sick if she doesn't watch what she eats all the time. It means no pigging out on chocolate or candy (which is why Claudia always keeps some "good" junk food around for meetings, like pretzels or Frookies, which are cookies sweetened only with fruit juice). It also means she has to give herself shots of insulin every day to help regulate the sugar in her blood.

I don't know if I could do that, but Stacey is really good about it. And all that healthy eating means she stays in shape, too. Which, when combined with Stacey's New York City style, means that people sit up and take notice when she comes into the room. She's a sophisticated dresser, more than the rest of us (although Claudia has a real style of her own, too). Furthermore, underneath that long, blonde hair is a brain that not only understands math, but likes it — which of course is why Stacey is our treasurer.

Our vice-president, and Stacey's best friend, is Claudia Kishi, who are both opposite in some ways, and alike in others.

Claudia, as I mentioned earlier, has style, too. But unlike Stacey's smooth city look, Claudia's style is a little more quirky and artsy. For instance, she painted her sneakers with her own personal designs. People notice Claud when she comes into a room, too. She's Japanese-American and really striking, with her long black hair and perfect complexion.

The differences between Claudia and Stacey? Well, take Claudia's complete appreciation of some of the worst junk food in the world, which Stacey can't eat. And while Stacey is a math whiz, Claudia would rate school as just one step above punishment. She's very creative — she's going to be an artist, probably a famous one someday — but Claudia's kind of creativity just doesn't translate into good grades in math or English (although her spelling is definitely creative). What's particularly hard for Claudia is that her sister, Janine, is a real, live genius.

Actually, Mr. and Mrs. Kishi do appreciate Claudia's talent. But they don't always understand her — how she could passionately love to read Nancy Drew books (she likes them as much as junk food, *and* she keeps them hidden around her room because her parents sort of equate eating junk food with reading those mysteries).

Jessica Ramsey and Mallory Pike, who are junior officers in the BSC, are another set of best friends who are alike in some ways, yet very different. They're junior officers because they're eleven years old, two years younger than the rest of us, and in the sixth grade. They can't take baby-sitting jobs that require them to work late at night, so they handle mostly after-school and weekend day clients, which frees the rest of us up for late-night sitting. Both Mal and Jessi are the oldest kids in their families, which means they have plenty of built-in baby-sitting experience. In fact, Mal has seven younger brothers and sisters (three of her brothers are triplets). Jessi has a younger sister and brother.

Both Jessi and Mallory are creative, but in entirely different ways. Jessi wants to be a prima ballerina someday, and she's already made a good start. She studies with a special teacher and she's even danced in real ballets.

Mal wants to be a children's book author and illustrator. She writes and illustrates wonderful stories.

Both Mal and Jessi love to read. And they both feel that, as the oldest kids in their families, they should be treated more like adults and less like the rest of the kids. They took a step in that direction (and passed me!) recently when they were allowed to have their ears pierced.

Physically, they're pretty different, too. Jessi looks and stands and walks the way I imagine a prima ballerina does. She has an extra sort of grace, and she's incredibly limber. She has dark brown skin, brown eyes, and doesn't wear glasses or braces — both of which Mal has.

Mal doesn't have Jessi's tall elegance. She's more average, I guess, except that she has wonderful curly red hair, pale skin, and blue eyes.

Our two associate members, Shannon Kilbourne and Logan Bruno, are available to take on jobs we can't fit in. They're *not* best friends with each other. In fact, they don't even attend meetings as a rule, although Shannon Kilbourne has been coming more often lately.

Shannon is a neighbor of Kristy's who goes to Stoneybrook Day School, which is a private school. Kristy's family's dog, a Bernese Mountain dog, is named after Shannon, because Shannon gave Kristy one of her dog's puppies when the Thomases' wonderful old collie, Louie, died. Kristy still wears a baseball cap with a collie on the front of it.

Logan Bruno. Logan. Well, he's pretty special. That's what I think, and not only because he's a guy who knows how to handle a baby-sitting job as well as the usual sports things guys do. I mean, Kristy can do that, too. No, Logan is special because — he's my boyfriend. In fact, I would think he was special even if he weren't.

For one thing, he is major cute, even cuter than Cam Geary (although they do look alike), who is my favorite movie star.

And he — Logan — has a great Southern accent and a way of really listening to you when you talk to him. It's funny. I am the shyest and most sensitive of all my friends, and the only one with a steady boyfriend. But most of the time, I like having Logan as my boyfriend.

Most of the time, but not all of the time? Well, Logan can be a little bossy. In fact, not long after we started going out, he started making decisions for both of us, planning things for us without talking to me first, as if he assumed that because I was shy, I didn't have an opinion. I did, though. And we broke up for awhile because Logan didn't understand how I felt.

But we really missed each other, so we decided to try things out again. And so far, I've been really glad we did.

So that's the BSC, all nine of us. We've become a successful business with regular clients who give us good recommendations. They're so good, in fact, that we rarely need to distribute fliers or put signs up in supermarkets anymore. And like any good business we have officers, rules, records, and dues.

We even have a place of business where we keep regular hours: Claudia's, on Mondays, Wednesdays, and Fridays from five-thirty to six. During the meetings we book appointments, collect dues (on Mondays), and generally take care of business.

Since Claud is our vice-president and the only one of us with her own phone line, it's ideal. That way, our line isn't tied up with anyone else's phone calls when clients are trying to reach us, and we aren't tying up anybody else's phone with our business calls, either.

So you see, we are all very different (I guess that means that happy baby-sitters clubs aren't all alike, either) but we have a lot in common. And with so many different ways of thinking and seeing, and so many talents available, it was only natural that I should turn to the BSC for some help in figuring out how to meet Mrs. Towne.

Kristy, who'd managed to listen while I described baby-sitting for the Arnolds, to remind me not to forget to write it up in the BSC notebook, to negotiate more money for new supplies for the Kid-Kit with Stacey, *and* to answer the phone, said as she hung up, "Why didn't you just knock on Mrs. Towne's door?"

"Uh," I said, writing Mal in for an afternoon job on Thursday.

"Well?" said Kristy.

I finished what I was doing (I can only do one thing at a time, but I have never, ever made a mistake in scheduling) and looked at Kristy. "Just knock on Mrs. Towne's door? I don't think so, Kristy."

"Why not?"

I gave Kristy a Look. However, Kristy is one of the few people I know who will argue with a Look. She said, "But how are you ever going to meet Mrs. Towne if you don't, Mary Anne? If you're really shy, I could come with you . . ."

"Thanks," I said helplessly, "but I just can't

walk up to someone's door and knock and then ask them to give me sewing lessons, okay, Kristy?"

Kristy looked stubborn, but before she could argue, Claudia said sensibly, "Why don't you call her, Mary Anne?"

"Excellent," said Kristy.

The phone rang. Kristy picked it up and said, "Baby-sitters Club . . . Yes. Hello, Mrs. Pike. No, I'm sorry, I don't know if Mal is free then, but of course we have a number of other baby-sitters who might be available Thursday if she isn't. Yes, I know it's a two-person sitting job. Okay, I'll call you right back.

"Mrs. Pike needs someone for next Thursday afternoon from three-thirty until five. She requested Mallory."

Mallory grinned, and I hid a smile at how formal Kristy sounded. "Let me check," I said, trying to sound equally formal. "Hmmm. Well, Mal's available, I'm available, and Dawn, you're available."

Dawn, who'd been sort of quiet during the meeting, shook her head slightly. "Mary Anne, you and Mal take it."

"Are you sure?" I asked.

"Sure," said Dawn.

"Okay." I carefully wrote it in the book while Kristy called Mrs. Pike back and gave her the information.

Jessi looked down at her Swatch. "Six o'clock," she informed us.

Kristy checked her watch and frowned. "I have 5:59."

We knew better than to argue. We waited. Then Kristy said, "Six o'clock. This meeting of the BSC is officially adjourned."

It had been an uneventful meeting. But as Dawn and I walked home together, I felt pleased. "Why didn't I think of just calling Mrs. Towne?" I wondered aloud. "That would be okay, don't you think, Dawn?"

"That would be fine. In fact, Mrs. Towne will probably be flattered by your interest."

As it turned out, Dawn was right. I gathered my courage after dinner and found Mrs. Towne's number in the phone book. In a rush I told her who I was, and that Mrs. Stone had suggested I call because I love to sew.

For a moment, the other end was quiet. Then Mrs. Towne said, "Mary Anne, I'm flattered. Why don't you come by for a visit and we'll talk."

"Really?" I said.

"I'd love it."

"Well, ah, what's a good time for you?"

"Oh, any time is fine. Why not tomorrow afternoon?"

I did a quick mental check: no baby-sitting,

no trips to dentists or doctors. And no homework, of course.

"I'd like that," I told Mrs. Towne.

"Come about four o'clock and we'll have a cup of tea," said Mrs. Towne.

"Thank you," I replied. "See you tomorrow."

I hung up and raced to Dawn's room. Dawn was lying on the bed, her hands folded under her head. An old album by the Beach Boys was playing. I shook my head.

"Do you really wish they could all be California girls?" I teased her.

Dawn sighed and sat up. "No," she said. "But I miss it a lot, these days."

"Hey, it's summer in Stoneybrook. Nice and hot. Not *too* far from the beach."

Dawn smiled a little. "It's warmer. But I wouldn't call it hot."

I laughed. "Guess what? Mrs. Towne invited me over tomorrow to talk about sewing. Isn't that great?"

"It really is, Mary Anne," said Dawn.

"Should I take some of my sewing? What would you do, Dawn? You know, you were exactly right about her being flattered. She even said so."

"That's great," said Dawn. She reached over and turned the music off. "Come on and sit down."

Still talking about Mrs. Towne, I made myself comfortable at the foot of Dawn's bed. We talked until Sharon came up to tell us that, summer or no summer, we had to go to sleep.

"In California, it's three hours earlier," said Dawn.

"We're not in California anymore," said Sharon, grinning. "Come on, Mary Anne, Dawn."

"Too bad we're not in California, then, isn't it, Dawn?" I said getting up. "Good night."

"Good night," said Dawn. As I left the room, I thought I heard her reach over and turn the Beach Boys back on, very softly.

CHAPTER 3

I knocked on Mrs. Towne's door at exactly four o'clock the next afternoon. To keep from being *too* nervous, I was trying to pretend I was knocking on the door of a new client for the BSC. Thinking of myself as Mary Anne Spier, baby-sitter, was easier than Mary Anne Spier, stranger-standing-at-the-door.

When Mrs. Towne didn't answer right away, I thought she'd forgotten. Or maybe she'd changed her mind. I raised my hand. I looked down at my feet. Should I knock again? Or run away instead?

Fortunately, the door opened just then and Mrs. Towne took my upraised hand in hers as if it were perfectly normal to find someone standing at the door with her hand raised to shoulder height as if she were about to wave (or knock). She gave me a quick, formal handshake, saying as she did, "Mary Anne Spier?"

"Yes. Uh, Mrs. Towne?" Inside I groaned.

33

What a dumb question. Who else would be answering Mrs. Towne's door?

But Mrs. Towne didn't seem to think it was dumb. She nodded, smiling, and stepped back for me to come in.

I don't know what I'd expected Mrs. Towne to be like — maybe an apple-cheeked little old lady swathed in a big apron with her hair in a grandmotherly bun. Or maybe someone in a long, old-fashioned dress wearing one of those wrist pincushions stuck full of pins, peering nearsightedly (from all those hours spent sewing) at me through big glasses. Whatever it was, Mrs. Towne wasn't quite what I'd pictured.

She was small, hardly any taller than I. But she wasn't a storybook grandmotherly type with apple cheeks and a big apron. She had sharp, direct brown eyes and very short white hair that looked almost punk. Her skin was pale brown and smooth and soft, so that if it hadn't been for her white hair, you wouldn't have had any idea how old she might be.

No apron either. She was wearing jeans and a blue work shirt and tennis shoes.

Her house was more what I expected. Or at least, it was sort of familiar to me, because I could see as I stepped inside the door that it was an old farmhouse like ours, with low ceilings and stairs leading from the front hall, the same as in our house.

The familiarity made me feel less nervous. I began to relax.

"I've been looking forward to your visit," said Mrs. Towne in a soft voice as she led the way down the hall. "I've set up tea on the back porch. It's a nice view from there."

We walked through a big, sunny, old-fashioned kitchen and out onto an even sunnier porch filled with plants of all kinds and sizes. At one end of the porch was a white table with two white chairs pulled up to it. On the table was a teapot, a bowl of sugar, a little pitcher of milk, a bowl of lemon slices, a plate of cookies, a saucer with a silver strainer not much bigger than a tablespoon, and two places set with cups and saucers, small plates, and teaspoons on top of neatly folded napkins.

"I had just taken the kettle off when you knocked," explained Mrs. Towne, motioning me to one of the chairs. "I poured the hot water into the teapot before I answered the door, so the tea should be just about right. Do you like tea?"

Logan, who is from the South, drinks iced tea all the time, and Dawn drinks hot herb tea in the winter, but I'd never really thought about it. I nodded anyway.

"Oh, good," said Mrs. Towne. She put a little silver strainer on top of my cup and poured the tea into it, then did the same with her cup. She set the strainer, which had loose tea leaves in it, on a separate plate. "This is chamomile tea. I made it from my own chamomile flowers."

Fortunately, I'd heard of chamomile tea. It was one of the teas Dawn drank.

Mrs. Towne said, "Sugar? Milk or lemon?"

I put two teaspoons of sugar in the tea (something Dawn *never* would have done) and took a sugar cookie from the plate when Mrs. Towne offered it.

The tea was very hot, but it was good. I sipped it slowly, looking around the porch. I'd half expected to see samples of Mrs. Towne's work everywhere, but the sun porch didn't have room for anything, not even more plants.

"The way the porch is designed," said Mrs. Towne, following my thoughts, "I'm able to use it as a sort of greenhouse for starting seedlings, even in the winter. The windows are all around, you see, and they slide open in the summer to let the warm air in through the screens. In the winter, they slide shut and I put up storm windows and open the heating vent. That way I have sun and warmth all year round."

"That's great," I said, reminded again of

Dawn. Would she think having a sun porch was almost as good as being in California? Somehow I didn't think so.

"Have you been sewing long?" asked Mrs. Towne.

"I've always liked it," I said, "but it wasn't until recently that I really started to get interested in it." (I decided not to mention the slight problem I'd had with home ec class.)

"My grandmother taught me how to sew," said Mrs. Towne. "I was just a little girl. She could hand stitch a hem as fine as any sewing machine I've ever seen. She took in sewing for a living, and although we never had much money, I was always the best-dressed girl in school."

"She made all your clothes by hand?" I asked incredulously.

"Lord, yes." Mrs. Towne laughed. "We all grew up sewing. We'd sit at night and talk and sew, when there weren't other chores to do, of course. It was wonderful."

It sounded hard to me. And what if Mrs. Towne looked down on people who used sewing machines? I said, cautiously, "I'm just learning to embroider. I've read about French hand sewing. And I'd like to learn smocking, and more about sewing, too. But I've done most of my sewing on a machine."

"Well, I don't blame you!" said Mrs. Towne. "Times have changed. Sewing machines are great labor-saving devices. Although you still have to do some things by hand."

"I know," I said, relieved. I put down my empty cup.

"More tea?"

"Not right now, thank you," I said. I suddenly realized that the teapot was wearing a little quilted coat.

"Did you make that?" I asked.

"The tea cozy? Yes, I did. It's very old, almost as old as I am. It was one of my first quilting efforts, with my grandmother. Two layers of flannel — one of my father's old flannel shirts, with cotton batting in between. It helps the tea stay warm inside the pot."

"Like insulation," I said.

"Exactly," said Mrs. Towne. She put her own teacup down and stood up. "Why don't I show you where I work and some of the other things I've done?"

"I'd love that," I said truthfully. Now that I felt comfortable with Mrs. Towne, I could hardly wait to see her work.

I followed Mrs. Towne back out to the hall. She opened a door. "This is the guest room," she said. "And this . . ."

"You made that," I said. Spread across the bed was the most beautiful quilt I had ever seen.

"The pattern is called Log Cabin. It's an Amish pattern. The center of each of the squares is red because that symbolizes the hearth of the cabin: fire and warmth and where the meals are cooked."

"It's beautiful," I said. I walked over to the bed. "May I touch it?"

"Lord, yes! It won't break."

I bent over and ran my hand over the quilted surface. The detail of the quilting — the stitching that sewed the front of the blanket to the back of the blanket — was intricate and precise.

Looking up the bed, I realized that the pillows were edged with the most delicate embroidery, white thread against the white cotton. "That, too?" I asked.

She nodded, smiling.

Mrs. Towne's handiwork was evident in almost every room of the house: a footstool with a tapestry design worked into the top, the invisible hem on the fluted edge of a curtain — and a quilt in every room, either hanging on a wall, or spread across a bed.

Then we went into a large room on the front corner of the house. From the windows I could see the road and down the hill to the Stones' farm.

"This is my workroom," said Mrs. Towne.

I stepped into the middle of the room and looked around in awe.

Although the room was big, you wouldn't have realized it right away, because it was so full. To one side was a quilting frame, with what looked like a crazy quilt stretched across the top of it. Two dressmaker's dummies, one large and one small, stood in a corner. A rack on the wall behind the dummies held, among other things, several pairs of scissors and shears in various sizes with straight and serrated edges, an assortment of embroidery hoops, a pattern-tracing wheel and a couple of tape measures, and various sewing rulers, curved and straight. A pattern, made of plain tissue paper, with various markings on it in pencil, was pinned to a piece of rose-printed material laid out on a large table. A sewing machine stood in a niche of its own by the window, with a sewing box on legs next to it. The top of the box was open and inside I could see, neatly arranged, dozens and dozens of spools of thread of all kinds and colors. A chest of drawers made up of many tiny drawers stood against one wall. Each drawer was labeled, and I realized that inside were various buttons, trims, pipings, beads, and all sorts of other sewing paraphernalia.

It was awesome.

"This is awesome," I breathed, and then

blushed, afraid Mrs. Towne would think I was weird.

But to my surprise she laughed. "That's a nice way of putting it! My son, Cal — he lives in Missouri — calls it terrifying. But I know exactly where everything is. I ought to. I've been working in this room for years!"

"A pleater?" I asked. I pointed to a small machine with a row of needles on it. A piece of material was between the rollers behind the needles, waiting to be rolled through.

"Not everybody would know that!" laughed Mrs. Towne. "Do you have one?"

"No," I said. "We just have the basic equipment. You know, a sewing machine, darning and crewel needles, some shears, and a pair of scissors."

"Here, let me show you how it works." Mrs. Towne sat down at the pleater and pulled a chair up next to her.

I was in sewing heaven.

Using the pleater wasn't as hard as I thought it would be. After that, Mrs. Towne showed me some basic smocking and what she called "easy techniques for French hand sewing by machine." It wasn't *that* easy, but it was fascinating.

"You have a talent for this," said Mrs. Towne as we were finishing up.

"Do you think . . . I mean, would it be

possible for you to give me some lessons?" I asked.

To my surprise, Mrs. Towne said instantly, "What a wonderful idea, Mary Anne."

"I'd pay you, of course," I hurried on.

"When do you want to begin?" asked Mrs. Towne.

"I don't know. What's a good time for you? You have so much work. You must have a very busy schedule."

"Don't worry about that," Mrs. Towne told me. "What about next Saturday afternoon? We could have a lesson and then tea."

As Mrs. Towne walked me to the door, we worked out the details. I was so excited I practically levitated all the way home. I could hardly wait for next Saturday to come, to see more of Mrs. Towne's work, and to begin to learn how to sew like she did.

I didn't have to wait until Saturday to see Mrs. Towne, though. On Thursday afternoon I was baby-sitting for the younger Pike kids: Vanessa, Nicky, Claire, and Margo, and we went on another goat-visiting expedition.

I know, I know, it's not the usual baby-sitting activity, but as it happened, Elvira Goat has been the star of a play written by Vanessa and performed by the Pike kids when she was being goat-sat by Dawn and me. So it was only natural that they'd want to visit their leading lady. Or maybe I mean their leading goat.

Of course, the visit was a huge success. Even chewing on the garbage *du jour* (that's French for "of the day") Elvira is terminally cute.

After the visit, as we were walking home talking about goats (what else?) a voice called to us and I looked up to see Mrs. Towne by one of the flower beds, holding a spade and wearing gloves and a baseball cap.

"Mary Anne?"

"Mrs. Towne! Hi! We were just on our way back from visiting the Stones' farm."

"And Elvira Goat," called Claire importantly.

"Ah, yes. Mrs. Stone has told me about Elvira," said Mrs. Towne.

"Do you like goats?" asked Claire.

"I do," said Mrs. Towne. She and Claire exchanged smiles of mutual approval and then Mrs. Towne said, "Would you like to come in for a little while?"

I hesitated. I thought Mrs. Towne's house was possibly the most wonderful place on earth, but I wasn't sure what the Pikes would make of it.

As it turned out, I needn't have worried. They seemed as fascinated as I had been. When Vanessa saw the Log Cabin quilt and heard the story of its pattern, she narrowed her eyes and studied it thoughtfully. Vanessa's career plans (she's nine) are to be a poet. I could see that the idea for a poem was germinating in her mind.

Nicky was more direct. "Cool," he said to Mrs. Towne. "Are there more?" He plied her with questions about every quilt. His favorite, not surprisingly, was a finished crazy quilt displayed on the living room wall.

But to my amazement, the workroom enthralled them almost as much as it had me. I had noticed the children's clothes patterns on my first visit, but I hadn't looked closely at them. Vanessa, however, did, and was instantly in love with the picture smocking that decorated some of them, including scenes from fairy tales. Soon she was pointing out the various characters on a series of pillows Mrs. Towne was making, explaining them to Margo as if she had made them herself. Meanwhile, Nicky and Claire had gravitated to the quilting frame. Nicky bent over to look under it. "It's just sitting on sawhorses," he said.

"That's right. The frame is used to stretch the top of the quilt out so you can sew the middle and the bottom to it. That's the part that is called quilting — putting the three pieces together. This frame is a homemade frame. You can buy them, of course, but there's no need to. My husband made that one for me." For a moment, the bright, friendly look left Mrs. Towne's face and she seemed sad, but Nicky's next question brought it back.

"Do you have to know special stuff to make quilts?"

"No. At least I don't think so. You can buy patterns for most of them. But even with patterns, you have to plan very carefully. . . . You know, a lot of these patterns are Amish patterns, which is why they are so abstract. The Amish aren't allowed to show figures or any kind of realism in their quilting."

"Cool," said Nicky again. He reached out and gave the quilt a friendly pat.

And that gave me an idea.

We left soon after — the Pikes had to get home. I didn't say anything about my idea then. I wanted to think it over a little, and make sure it was as brilliant as I thought it was.

But I was pretty sure that it might possibly be one of those truly great, Kristy-caliber ideas. And if it was, I could hardly wait to tell my friends in the Baby-sitters Club.

CHAPTER 4

Asking Mrs. Towne for sewing lessons was supposed to be the hard part. After that, I wasn't going to be nervous at all. At least, that's what I thought. But by Saturday afternoon after lunch, I *was* nervous all over again.

I wasn't worried about seeing Mrs. Towne. I was looking forward to that. I could hardly wait to begin my sewing lessons.

But I couldn't make up my mind about what to take. At one o'clock I was ransacking my sewing box. Thread? Should I take thread? If so, what kind? How much? What color? And what about scissors? Mrs. Towne had plenty of scissors and shears, but maybe she didn't like for people to use her sewing equipment. Embroidery hoops? Samples of my own work?

Finally I settled on some black thread, some white thread, a paper of needles, a pair of scissors and a pair of shears, and a thimble.

Then I looked at the clock, and said (just like the White Rabbit in Alice in Wonderland) "I'm late, I'm late, I'm late!"

I biked at top speed all the way to Mrs. Towne's house. I wasn't late, but I was panting when I rang her doorbell exactly at two o'clock.

Fortunately, Mrs. Towne didn't come right away. I had time to catch my breath. Then I rang the doorbell again.

No one answered. I frowned. The doorbell was working. I could hear it. The screen door was shut but the front door behind it was open. I leaned forward and peered into the dim but now familiar hallway. I could see no sign of Mrs. Towne.

I rang the doorbell again.

But Mrs. Towne didn't appear.

Of course! She was probably gardening and couldn't even hear the doorbell. I put my makeshift sewing kit (it was an old canvas tote bag with a picture of a kitten on the front) on the porch, went down the stairs, and walked around to the back of the house.

The air was warm and the bees were making a drowsy buzzing sound among the hollyhocks and zinnias. But there was no sign of Mrs. Towne anywhere. To make sure, I walked back to the front porch from the other side of the house.

No Mrs. Towne.

Now what should I do? Had Mrs. Towne forgotten? I couldn't believe that she had. She had even reminded me of the lesson as I had left with the Pikes on Thursday afternoon. Besides, her car was still parked in the driveway.

I rang the bell once more, keeping my finger on it for a long time.

No one answered.

Now I was beginning to worry. Could something be wrong? Hesitantly, I tried the screen door. The knob turned easily. I pushed the door slowly open and stuck my head inside. "Hello, Mrs. Towne?" I called. "It's me, Mrs. Towne! Mary Anne Spier!"

I waited. I was just about to call again when I heard it. A thin sound, like a voice calling weakly.

"Hello?" I said again. "Mrs. Towne?"

"Help! Help me!"

Was I hearing right? With my heart pounding, I stepped through the door and walked down the silent, shadowy hall. "Hello?" I called again, and listened to the echo of my voice.

But it wasn't an echo that answered, faintly. "Here. In here . . ."

I began to run. A moment later, I skidded to a stop in the doorway of Mrs. Towne's big, old-fashioned kitchen. Around the corner of the kitchen table, I could see a pair of blue-jeaned legs. One of the feet was turned at a funny angle.

"Mrs. Towne? Mrs. Towne!" I gasped. I ran over and knelt down beside her.

"Mrs. Towne, it's me, Mary Anne Spier," I told her, trying to sound calm.

Mrs. Towne moved slightly, her eyelids fluttering, and murmured something.

"Don't move," I said. "I'll get help."

Quickly, with shaking hands, I went to the phone on the kitchen wall and dialed 911. "Someone has had an accident," I told the man who answered. I told them about Mrs. Towne and I gave him the address.

"Don't move her," he told me. "Cover her with a blanket. The paramedics will be there in a few minutes."

Mrs. Towne shifted slightly. A blanket, I thought.

"I'll be right back, Mrs. Towne," I said. I raced to the guest bedroom and pulled the Log Cabin quilt off the bed and took it back to spread over Mrs. Towne.

She didn't move. I watched her for a moment, then got up again, ran to the phone, and called my house. My father answered. Even though my hands were shaking, I was surprised to hear how calm I sounded. "Mrs. Towne has fallen, Dad. I'm with her at her house. We're waiting for the paramedics."

"I'm on my way," my father said.

As I hung up, Mrs. Towne moaned softly. "Don't move," I told her, kneeling down. "It's me. It's Mary Anne. I'm here. And the paramedics are on their way."

I smoothed the quilt over Mrs. Towne, then took her hand and settled down to wait.

I know it wasn't very long, but it seemed like forever before I heard the screen door bang open and footsteps in the hall. "Mary Anne?" my father's voice called.

I was *so* glad to hear it. "In here," I said. A moment later he stepped into the kitchen followed by the paramedics.

I gave Mrs. Towne's hand a reassuring pat, put it under the quilt, stood up, and stepped back.

One of the paramedics knelt by Mrs. Towne and took her pulse. "Has she been moved?" the paramedic asked me.

I shook my head. "I found her like this about ten minutes ago. I called 911 and then put the blanket over her."

The paramedic nodded. "Good," she told me and, pulling the blanket back, began to check Mrs. Towne.

My father put his hand on my shoulder and gave it a reassuring squeeze.

"It looks like a broken ankle," the first paramedic said, standing up. "I don't see anything else, but of course we won't know until we get her to the hospital."

"We'll follow you there," my father said as the paramedics lifted the stretcher with Mrs. Towne on it. I spread the quilt carefully back over the bed. My hands wouldn't stop shaking. I had to clutch them in my lap all the way to the hospital.

"You did a good job, Mary Anne," my father kept saying. But I couldn't believe it, at least not until I knew Mrs. Towne was going to be all right.

We waited a long time. At last a nurse led us down the hall of the emergency room.

Mrs. Towne was sitting in a wheelchair with her ankle propped up and a big cast around it.

"Mrs. Towne? Are you okay?"

She smiled ruefully. "Fine, except for this darned old ankle. Mary Anne, I'm so glad you came over today. Thank you for everything."

I felt myself blushing. "You're welcome, Mrs. Towne. I'm glad I could help. But what happened?"

"I don't know. One minute I was walking across the kitchen floor and the next minute I was lying on it. I must have slipped and then passed out from the pain. They tell me my ankle is badly broken. But I'm lucky, I suppose, that it is nothing worse."

"Does it hurt now?"

Mrs. Towne nodded. "Yes, but not as badly as it did. I'll be in the hospital for a few days, then I'll be sort of immobile for awhile." She made a face and I could see the thought of being immobile bothered her almost as much as having a broken ankle.

"Is there anything I can do? Do you want someone to get in touch with your son?"

Mrs. Towne thought for a moment, then shook her head. "I'll call him later, but there's no sense in worrying him. He can't do anything for me long distance. I'll ask Mrs. Stone to keep an eye on my garden and my mail while I'm away. She has a spare key to my house that I gave her a long time ago in case of emergencies. She can bring me anything I need, too."

A nurse bustled over to us and smiled at us. "How are we feeling?" he asked.

"*I'm* feeling fine," said Mrs. Towne. "I can't answer for Mary Anne, of course."

I hid a smile. Mrs. Towne might have a broken ankle, but she wasn't about to let a nurse treat her like an invalid!

The nurse looked taken aback, then he smiled, too. "Good," he said. "Your room is ready for you. Are you ready to go?"

"I suppose so," said Mrs. Towne.

"I'll come visit soon," I promised.

"Thank you, Mary Anne," said Mrs. Towne. She leaned her head back against the wheelchair and closed her eyes. "I am feeling a *little* tired," she admitted.

The nurse nodded and said to me, "Room two-eleven. It's a semi-private room on the second floor. Visiting hours are from three to four-thirty in the afternoon and from seven until eight-thirty at night."

"Thank you," I said. "Good-bye, Mrs. Towne."

"Good-bye, Mary Anne," she said, her eyes still closed.

She suddenly did sound tired. Poor Mrs. Towne. Her son was far away and she was all alone. I thought of the times I'd felt sorry for myself and gave myself a mental shake. You see, I scolded myself. You have it easy, Mary Anne Spier.

As Mrs. Towne's wheelchair disappeared down the hall, I resolved to be as unselfish and helpful as I could for her. And I was going to start by visiting her the very next day. I'd bring her the Log Cabin quilt for her bed. Maybe that would help to cheer her up.

CHAPTER 5

On Wednesday, Dawn and I decided to ride our bicycles to Claudia's house for the BSC meeting. I'm not much of an athlete the way Kristy is, but I do like riding my bike. So Dawn and I raced up and down the hills to Claudia's house.

We burst in the door, shrieking and laughing like crazy (the Kishis always leave the door open on meeting afternoons) and ran right into Claudia's sister, Janine the genius.

She raised her eyebrows at us. Janine can be pretty cool sometimes, but she can also be an older-sister-type pain and make you wonder if she and Claudia are actually related. Today she was clearly in her older-sister mode.

"Janine, hey. What's happening!" said Dawn, still gasping for breath.

"You lost," I declared.

"Huh!" said Dawn.

"I suppose you are vying for victory in some sort of contest," said Janine.

"Yeah, we had a bicycle race," replied Dawn, correctly interpreting what Janine had just said. "Mary Anne cheated."

Janine looked shocked, which made me laugh harder.

"Only by California rules, Dawn," I said. "In Stoneybrook, it is perfectly legal to say, 'Your rear tire is flat.' "

"Was it?" asked Janine.

I looked innocent. "Maybe."

Dawn elbowed me. "Yeah, right. And by the time I stopped to look, you'd gone ahead!"

"Safety first," I said loftily, running up the stairs.

"A BSC motto, no doubt," said Janine dryly.

Dawn laughed, and so did I, and Janine permitted herself a small smile.

We were right on time. As we walked in, Claudia made an overhand pass with the bag of Gummi worms she was holding, and Dawn caught it in one hand and passed it off to me.

Kristy said, "This meeting of the . . ." and the phone rang.

"Baby-sitters Club," filled in Stacey, picking up the phone. I pulled out the record book and flipped it open as Stacey repeated the information and said she'd call back.

"Mrs. Papadakis," she announced. "Friday afternoon from two until six."

I studied the record book and then said, "It's pretty open — Kristy, Claudia, or Jessi."

Jessi said, "Count me out. Mal and I are vidding out on Friday."

"Vidding out?" asked Stacey. "As in, videos?"

"Yup." Mal grinned. "Horse-o-rama."

"*National Velvet* again?" groaned Claudia.

"And *The Black Stallion*," said Jessi, unperturbed.

In case you can't tell, Jessi and Mal are fond of horses, to put it mildly.

"You take it, Kristy," said Claudia. "You're right across the street from the Papadakises, so it's more convenient."

"Okay," said Kristy, and I wrote her in.

As soon as Stacey had hung up the phone after calling Mrs. Papadakis back, it rang again. And then again. It was shaping up to be a pretty busy meeting for a summer afternoon. Soon every one of us had lined up at least one job for the next week — except me.

"The twins," said Kristy, looking at me. "Tomorrow afternoon? They're near you, Mary Anne."

I looked in the book and almost agreed. But

then I remembered. "I can't," I said. "Mrs. Towne may be getting out of the hospital tomorrow. I want to be free to visit her. But Dawn and Mallory have openings."

"You do it, Mal," said Dawn. "It'll help pay for your vidding."

We all laughed and I wrote Mal in.

"How *is* Mrs. Towne, anyway?" Stacey asked me.

"Well, her ankle is healing fine, but it might be a while before she's walking around again. Sometimes when you're older, it takes longer for things to heal."

"She's been in the hospital a long time," said Jessi. "Is that why?"

I shook my head. "Not exactly. She probably could have gone home sooner, but since she lives alone, she decided to stay a couple of extra days. She says in the hospital she doesn't have to cook or clean or go up and down the stairs."

"Wow, that's right," said Claudia. "What's she going to do when she gets home?"

"A visiting nurse is going to come to her house once a day to help with medication and check on her ankle for awhile," I said. "And Mrs. Stone has moved things from Mrs. Towne's bedroom upstairs to the guest bedroom downstairs so she doesn't have to go up and down any steps. Plus, I'm going to go over or call as much as I can, and try to help out."

"Decent," said Stacey.

"Yeah," said Kristy. "But what about your sewing lessons?"

"She still wants to give them to me, so we're going to start this Saturday instead. Meanwhile, I had a good — no, a great — idea. I think."

Kristy immediately looked enthusiastic. She loves ideas, even when they aren't her own. "What?"

"I've been thinking about this ever since I visited Mrs. Towne's with your brothers and sisters last Wednesday, Mal."

"They liked that a lot," said Mal. "A farm, a goat, and Mrs. Towne's house all in one day. Vanessa and Nicky are still talking about those quilts."

"That's it," I said. "That's the idea. I was wondering if some of the kids we sit for would like sewing lessons, too. Nothing fancy, like Mrs. Towne is going to teach me, but you know, fun stuff. Like designing a simple quilt or something like that. I've been looking through a few quilting books and it wouldn't be hard."

"Definitely decent," said Stacey.

"And that's definitely a great idea," Kristy

agreed. "Let's make a few phone calls and see."

I knew I could count on my friends. With Kristy making the calls, we'd "enrolled" six kids in my sewing class by the time the meeting was over. Vanessa and Nicky Pike, Becca Ramsey, Charlotte Johanssen, Buddy Barrett, and Haley Braddock.

It happened so fast, it almost took my breath away. If you ever want something to happen, Kristy is the one to help you out.

I looked up and caught Dawn's eye and smiled. She gave me a thumbs-up sign.

"Now if we were in California," she said, "Jeff would probably like to take your class, too."

"And make a surfboard cover," teased Stacey.

We all laughed, including Dawn.

"Hey, Dawn," said Kristy, looking out the window and reaching up for her visor. "This is perfect weather, right here in Stoneybrook. You can't possibly miss California on a day like today."

Dawn didn't make a quick comeback, like I'd expected. Instead, she said, "Not California, so much. But I do miss Jeff and Dad."

We were all quiet for a moment and then I

said cheerfully, "But you'll get to see them soon, probably."

"Right," said Kristy. "Visit them in the winter when we're all freezing. You'll like that . . . Okay. This meeting of the BSC is officially adjourned."

We trooped out and Dawn and I pedaled home more slowly than we'd ridden over. On the way, I told her a little about the research I'd been doing on patchwork quilts. "Take the abstract designs used by the Amish. The names tell you where those designs come from in their everyday life, like 'Sunshine and Shadow' or 'Streak of Lightning.' "

"Hmm," said Dawn, lifting her face to the sun. " 'Sunshine and Shadow.' That sounds like a nice one."

"It is. You should see it! And listen to this . . ."

I was awfully excited about the sewing class. And I could hardly wait for my next sewing lesson. Also, I was glad to be doing something unselfish, glad to be able to help Mrs. Towne out.

Dawn didn't say much after that. I guess I didn't let her. Looking back, I think maybe I didn't want her to say anything too positive about California. Dawn belonged here, in Stoneybrook. I was afraid if she kept talking about California, she'd become really, truly homesick and want to go back.

It didn't occur to me until much, much later that the tone of voice I'd been using with Dawn whenever she talked about California and being homesick was a lot like the tone of voice the nurse had used with Mrs. Towne.

CHAPTER 6

Thursday

Ok. I'm totally ~~psyched~~ ~~syked~~ ~~sikpd~~ getting into this sowing stuff. Mary Anne, why didn't you tell me about quiltting and all that stuff before? I can see it has real potenshul for my art. I had allmost as much fun at Mary Anne's first sowing class as the kids did...

M_y first sewing class was scheduled for Thursday afternoon. With six kids, I figured I'd need help, so I asked for volunteers. Claudia decided it might be worth checking out, especially when she heard about the idea of designing quilts.

We met at my house. It was another perfect day in Stoneybrook, so I took an old bedspread outside and spread it under a tree in the yard for us. I'd suggested the kids each find a shoebox to make a sewing kit, and bring it along with a pair of blunt scissors, a box of pins, a package of needles, a spool of white thread, a thimble, and a few scraps of material for practicing on.

Meanwhile, I'd gathered my own boxful of materials (a box snow boots had come in, which was a little bigger). In it I'd put scraps of fabric and trimming, bits of lace, beads, and a couple of my sewing books plus the quilting books I'd checked out of the library. I'd also brought my own sewing box, of course, a real one designed for holding sewing things. I felt that I was prepared for anything.

As soon as everyone had arrived, we sat down on the bedspread. I'd decided we needed to run a basic skills check before we did anything else. I told each of them — Vanessa and Nicky, Becca, Charlotte, Buddy, and

Haley — to take out a needle and some thread.

"What size needle?" asked Charlotte. She held up not one but two packets of needles. One held sewing needles. The other held larger embroidery needles.

"One of those," I said, pointing to the regular ones. "We're going to start with how to thread needles."

"Ah, I know how to do that," said Nicky.

I smiled. "Good. Then you can help me show anybody who doesn't."

"Okay," he agreed.

Nicky, Vanessa, Charlotte, and Buddy knew how to thread needles and knot one end of the thread. Becca and Haley caught on right away. We progressed quickly from that to sewing a basic running stitch on the scraps of material.

"It's like that riddle," said Vanessa suddenly.

"Which riddle?" asked Charlotte. Her tongue was between her teeth and she was frowning at the material she was holding.

Vanessa dropped her sewing, clasped her hands together, and recited dramatically, "Old Mother Twitchett/has but one eye /and a long tail/which she can let fly /And every time she goes over a gap /she leaves a bit of her tail in a trap."

"I don't get it," said Charlotte.

"It's a *riddle*," said Vanessa. "With clues in the middle. You're supposed to guess. I cannot confess."

"Oh," said Charlotte.

No one said anything.

"Well," said Vanessa. "Tell. What is it? I'm caught in the middle. What's the answer to the riddle?"

"A snake?" said Haley. "A big, mean, one-eyed snake with one of those lizard tails like we studied in school? If you catch one of those lizards by the tail, it'll break off and the lizard will grow a new one."

"Really?" squealed Becca. "Euuw."

"*No!*" said Vanessa. "Guess again."

She looked around.

"Needle and thread," said Buddy Barrett without looking up.

Vanessa beamed. "Yes! Old Mother Twitchett is the needle, with one eye and the thread is her long tail. It's sort of poetic metaphor."

"We get it, Vanessa," said Nicky, not rudely, but firmly. Vanessa's poetic leanings include not only breaking into poetry at random intervals, but a fondness for words, especially when she was saying them.

Vanessa was as accustomed to Nicky as Nicky was to her, of course. She nodded and returned to her sewing.

I checked each person's progress (did I mention that Claudia could thread a needle and had a very nice running stitch?) and discovered that Charlotte knew some embroidery stitches.

"A chain stitch!" I said. "And a French knot. That's great, Charlotte."

She beamed. "I know how to make a fence stitch, too," she told me.

"Terrific. Do you think you could help me show those stitches to everyone else?"

"I think so," said Charlotte.

So after a basic sewing stitch, we began learning stitches for making pictures on cloth — embroidery. Everyone liked learning that as much as I remember I did when I first started sewing.

When the kids had filled up their scraps of material with running stitches and basting stitches and chain stitches and fence stitches and French knots, and had more or less mastered how to knot off the ends of the thread, I pulled out the sewing dictionary and the quilt books and passed them around.

"This is just to give you an idea of all the things you can sew. I was thinking we could work together on a project," I explained.

"Like a tapestry," Charlotte said. "We could embroider a really beautiful tapestry and hang it on a wall."

"Wow," said Claudia, flipping through a book of modern award-winning quilts. "These are awesome. Look at this one . . . it's sort of like Georgia O'Keefe meets Steven Spielberg's special effects guy."

"Can we make a quilt?" asked Vanessa. "Like the fairy-tale quilt in Mrs. Towne's house?"

"I don't want to do fairy tales," said Nicky. "I want to make a crazy quilt."

"I think a crazy quilt might be a little hard for us as beginners," I said. "I've never made a quilt, either, you guys, so I'll be learning along with you."

"What about a friendship quilt?" Claudia suggested.

"What's that?" asked Buddy.

"Ah, well, here's a picture of one. Mary Anne will explain."

I smiled at Claudia. "A friendship quilt is when people who are making the quilt each make a square or block, or even several blocks each. The blocks are all the same size but they can be different colors. Everyone makes a design on his or her block. Then the blocks are sewn together at the edges to make the top of the quilt."

"Oooh," said Vanessa. "I like that."

"Me, too," said Charlotte.

"Me three," said Nicky.

"How does everybody else feel?" I asked.

"Can we do anything we want on the blocks?" asked Buddy.

"Some quilts have a common theme, but I'd say yes, you can do anything you want." I wondered what Buddy had in mind. He didn't volunteer the information, though. He just nodded.

Becca and Haley liked the idea, too. We tossed around some ideas about the size of the squares, and how big the quilt would be and what kind of material we could use, and then the kids became a little wiggly. They'd been pretty good — we'd been sitting under the tree for over an hour, so I suggested we take a walk.

"May we go to Mrs. Towne's and see her quilts?" asked Vanessa. She turned to the others. "Mrs. Towne lives down the road and she has the most bea-uuutiful quilts."

"Can we, can we?" cried Becca and Haley.

"I don't see why not," I said. "Let me call Mrs. Towne first, though, and make sure it's okay."

"We'll clean up here," said Claudia.

Mrs. Towne sounded delighted to hear my voice. "Of course you can come over, Mary Anne. I'd love to have the company."

So a few minutes later, Claudia and the kids

and I were walking down the road to Mrs. Towne's house.

Mrs. Towne, leaning on her crutches, met us at the door. "I didn't want you to have to wait while I maneuvered these things down the hall," she explained. "They're as awkward as all get-out."

"I hope you feel better soon, Mrs. Towne," said Nicky.

"Why, thank you," replied Mrs. Towne.

"May we see your quilts?" asked Vanessa. "We're making a quilt, too."

"You are? Good for you. Come on, I'll show you everything."

With all the kids talking at once around her, Mrs. Towne made her way slowly down the narrow hall. It was hard for her to move without hitting the wall with one of her crutches. In the sewing room, Vanessa led the way straight to the fairy-tale quilt. "It's for a baby," she explained. "See? There's Humpty-Dumpty and there's Old Mother Goose and . . ."

"The Three Little Pigs," cried Haley.

"This is truly awesome," said Claudia softly. I nodded, but my mind wasn't really on the quilts. I'd noticed that Mrs. Towne's neat-as-a-pin house wasn't so neat anymore. The laundry room was heaped with laundry. And a quick glance in the kitchen had confirmed that dishes were piled in the sink and cans of food were sitting out on the kitchen table as if they'd been too hard to put away. Poor Mrs. Towne. With those crutches, it must have been very hard to do even the simplest things.

"I'll be back in a few minutes," I told Claudia softly. I slipped into the hall and went to the kitchen. I whisked the cans into the pantry, washed the dishes and set them in the drainer to dry, and wiped off the kitchen table and counters. There. At least Mrs. Towne wouldn't have to worry about that.

I met the others as they were coming out of the sewing room.

"I *love* your house, Mrs. Towne," said Vanessa. She gave a little skip. "Especially your quilts."

"Why, thank you." Mrs. Towne looked pleased.

"Thank you for letting us visit," I said. "It's time for us to go."

"Oh, must you?" said Mrs. Towne. "We could have some tea."

"Thank you, but it *is* getting late."

"Well, you are all welcome to visit any time," said Mrs. Towne.

"Thank you, Mrs. Towne," said Becca politely, and everyone else joined in.

Mrs. Towne waved from the door as we

hurried down the front walk and out to the road.

"That was cool," said Nicky.

"It really was," said Claudia.

"You think so?" I was truly pleased. I'd never imagined my sewing class idea would be a world-class, Kristy-caliber one. But it looked as if it were turning out that way.

CHAPTER 7

Saturday afternoon came at last. I was finally going to have my own private sewing lesson with Mrs. Towne. This time, after all that had happened, I wasn't nervous at all — even when it took Mrs. Towne a long time to come to the door. After all, I knew how clumsy those crutches were.

"Right on time," said Mrs. Towne. "In fact, you're a little ahead of me. I was going to be here waiting for you, but everything just takes so long with these darn crutches."

I nodded sympathetically. I couldn't think of anything to say.

Mrs. Towne didn't seem to notice. "The nurse helps, of course. But she'll only be coming for a few more days. Then I'll be on my own."

We went down the hall to the sewing room. It was a gray day, but the room was lit by old-fashioned floor lamps and it felt cozy and bright. Mrs. Towne lowered herself into a chair and hoisted her foot onto a footstool.

"Can I get you an extra pillow?" I asked.

"I'm fine, thanks. If you'll just pull up that chair over there. . . . Good."

In a few minutes we were settled down, and I was explaining to Mrs. Towne what I knew — and all that I *didn't* know — about sewing. "I'd like to learn more about embroidery. And about smocking. And I've read about French hand sewing, but I've never tried it," I confessed.

"Ah," said Mrs. Towne. "Well, I think you're more than ready to start on any or all of those things. And I have some books I can lend you that might be helpful, too."

"Great," I said happily.

I was enjoying myself so much I didn't realize how long we had been sitting until Mrs. Towne put down her smocking, stretched her arms, and twisted her neck from side to side. "I'm getting creaky, sitting here so long. What about some tea?"

"I'd like that," I said. "I never really drank tea before, but I liked yours."

"Good," said Mrs. Towne. She began to maneuver herself out of the chair.

"Can I help you?" I said anxiously. I thought she'd say no, she'd rather do it herself. I mean, Mrs. Towne struck me as the kind of independent person who *would* say that. But she surprised me by saying, "Yes, please."

And she leaned on me all the way to the kitchen, only using one crutch. I settled her in the kitchen chair and went back to get the other crutch. Then I put the tea kettle on.

"You should fill up the teapot with hot water," said Mrs. Towne. "That way when you put the tea in it and pour the boiling water out of the tea kettle over the leaves, the tea stays hotter longer. Tastes better, too."

"Okay. Where is the teapot?"

"Oh, dear. I'm afraid it's still out on the porch from when I had tea with the nurse. It's so hard to carry anything when you're on crutches."

"No problem," I said. "I'll get it." I went out to the porch and brought the teapot back in, rinsed the old tea out, washed the pot, and filled it with hot water. As I was setting out the cups and saucers, I noticed a bag of groceries sitting on the floor next to the counter. And I could see that the plants on the porch looked thirsty.

"Hasn't *anyone* been helping you?" I blurted out. Then I was embarrassed. Maybe Mrs. Towne would think I was saying her house was mess!

But she didn't take it that way.

"Well, as you know the nurse comes by. But she's really only supposed to check on my ankle and my medication. Besides, I can get around. I've been practicing using my canes. I'll switch from the crutches to the canes soon, and then I'll even be able to go up and down stairs."

I couldn't help but feel doubtful. Even with canes, it would be awhile before Mrs. Towne could get around as well as she had before. And if the laundry and the plants on the porch and the state of the kitchen were any indication, Mrs. Towne was going to have an overwhelming amount of work facing her when she was better.

The tea kettle began to sing and I jumped up to turn off the stove. Then I poured the hot water out of the teapot, spooned in the tea, poured the boiling water over the tea, and slipped the cozy over the pot. I carried it out to the porch and then helped Mrs. Towne.

When we were settled at the table on the porch, Mrs. Towne lifted the lid of the teapot and said, "About two more minutes, I'd say." She hesitated. "Mary Anne? Would you mind — I hate to ask you — but could you put the boxes in that grocery bag away in the pantry for me before you go?"

"Of course!" I'd seen that grocery bag sitting

there, I chided myself. How thoughtless of me to make Mrs. Towne ask. "I'll do it right now, while we wait for the tea."

"Are you sure?"

"No problem." I jumped up and put the groceries away, then returned to the table just as Mrs. Towne was pouring the tea.

We drank our tea and talked about gardening, and I told Mrs. Towne about the Baby-sitters Club. "Very enterprising," she said to me. "Very enterprising indeed. But then I'm not surprised. You strike me as a very smart, enterprising young woman."

That made me blush. But it felt good, too. I finished my tea and in a sort of whirl of energy and feeling-good, jumped up and cleared off the tea cups and saucers, washed the pot, and put everything away. Then I went to the back door, which was open onto the screen porch, and picked up the watering can just outside. "Why don't I water the plants on the porch?" I suggested.

"Oh, Mary Anne, thank you. They've been getting mighty thirsty and I just am not able to give them the attention they need."

I not only watered the plants, but I swept the porch and the kitchen. "The kitchen is probably ready to be mopped," I said tactfully (I hope). "You want me to just . . ."

"Oh, no, no, no. I couldn't . . ." Mrs.

Towne's voice trailed off and she looked at me thoughtfully. Then she said, "Mary Anne. Instead of paying me for sewing lessons in money, why don't we do some good, old-fashioned bartering?"

I understood immediately what she meant.

"That's a great idea, Mrs. Towne. That is, if you really think it is fair. I don't mind helping you a bit."

"I know you don't, but I'd feel much better if we did it this way. What do you think? Is it a deal?"

"It's a deal," I said.

"Great. Now, let's do a little more of the fun work — sewing — before the day is over."

"Why don't I put a load of laundry in while you get settled in the sewing room," I suggested. "Then I can put it in the dryer before I go."

"Perfect," said Mrs. Towne.

And that's the way I felt as I walked home after my sewing lesson. Perfect. It had been fun. I was learning new things. And I was going to be able to help Mrs. Towne, too.

Perfect. Just perfect.

CHAPTER 8

I'd decided to hold my sewing class on two afternoons a week, Tuesdays and Thursdays. Claudia had become my self-appointed permanent volunteer, and she was the first to arrive at the second class the next Tuesday.

"Look what I brought," she said, dumping her backpack on the chair in the den. She pulled out two books. "Janine found these at the library for me, under 'Folk Art.' I bet you never thought to look there!"

I hadn't. I shook my head.

"Yeah, me neither," said Claudia cheerfully. "Anyway, one of these books has a whole section on quilt projects by kids. You know what? Pioneer kids used to work on quilts all the time. It was part of their lives." She flipped through the pages. "See? Here's one signed in embroidery by a ten-year-old!"

"Cool," I said. We flipped through the pages and I was impressed. And inspired. So was Claudia. I could see new visions of Art filling her mind.

When the others arrived, Claudia's enthusiasm swept them up. The books and the project ideas were a smashing success. I'd never realized there were quite so many ways to look at — or make — a quilt. We saw dog quilts, with patches appliquéd with dogs, quilts that combined traditional patterns with outrageous modern materials like gold lamé and mylar, quilts that had been padded and stitched with patterns so that they were three dimensional, quilts that were so intricate they fooled the eye: one moment you thought you were looking at one picture, the next moment it had changed into something else. We saw quilts that used not only embroidery and appliqué techniques, but crocheting and knitting and even plastic and buttons and ceramic decorations. My favorite quilts were the ones that told stories and recorded history, such as the one called "Stars Fell on Alabama." It was about a night long ago when the skies over Alabama were filled with shooting stars.

And of course, every quilt we saw seemed better than the next. It took a long time to settle down and make final — and much less complicated — plans for our own quilt.

Claudia had brought over lots of plain paper and colored pencils. The patches in our quilt were going to be square, and the same size, so we traced one square several times and then handed the squares out to the kids. Claudia helped them draw the designs for their squares.

Claudia was a great help. Instead of telling the kids their designs were too complicated for even a very advanced quilter (Vanessa wanted to make Cinderella going to the ball on her square, embroidered with gold and silver), Claudia simply made the designs less complicated. For example, she suggested that Vanessa just show Cinderella's glass slippers, which could be cut out of silvery cloth and appliquéd onto a background. "Maybe we could make a pumpkin, too," suggested Claudia, "and put it here. What do you think? The orange would look good with the silver and it would be sort of a clue."

"A clue, a clue," sang Vanessa. "That's what I'll do." Which I guess meant, okay.

Then about halfway through the planning stage, Becca had a brilliant idea.

"Mary Anne?"

"Hmm?" I was frowning down at my piece of paper, which was blank, so far.

"We could make this quilt as a present for someone, couldn't we?"

"Sure, Becca. If everyone agrees."

"Then I think we should make it for Mrs. Towne. For a get-well present."

I put down my pencil. I felt myself choke up a little. I cleared my throat. "Becca, that's a *wonderful* idea. I wish I'd thought of it!" I did, too. Not only was it thoughtful and unselfish, but it solved the problem of who was going to get this quilt when we were done.

"A present for Mrs. Towne," sang Vanessa softly.

"All in favor say 'aye,' " I said.

The vote was unanimous.

"Then," said Becca, who'd obviously been thinking about this a lot, "we should make designs that Mrs. Towne would like. Shouldn't we, Mary Anne?"

"Did you have something in mind, Becca?"

Becca nodded. "Flowers. Mrs. Towne has a nice garden. If she had a quilt with flowers on it, it would be like having a garden inside. Each of us could make blocks with different flowers on them."

Buddy, who'd been drawing what I *think* was a football, said, "I don't want to make a quilt with old flowers on it."

"Maybe a more general theme, then," said Claudia. "Becca, what about a garden quilt? You know, you could show the different things you find in a garden, not just the flowers."

"Bugs!" cried Nicky.

I could tell Claudia was trying not to laugh, especially at the outraged look on Becca's face.

"And butterflies," I put in quickly.

"Hey! What about birds?" said Buddy. "Or a scarecrow? This'll be cool." He began to erase his piece of paper vigorously.

"We'll start over with new paper," said Claudia.

"I'm going to begin with a rose, I suppose," said Vanessa.

"Can I make a robin?" asked Haley anxiously. "Even though I don't think I can draw one exactly right?"

"Of course. Claudia can help you draw a robin," I told her. I wasn't surprised when Nicky picked a spider for the first of his blocks. But when Claudia suggested he make it on a blue piece of material and embroider a silver web for the spider, Nicky was even more pleased with his idea.

Charlotte decided to begin with a sunflower. Becca chose a butterfly.

"I'm going to try a watering can," said Claudia. "What about you, Mary Anne?"

"A tulip," I said. I like tulips. And it wouldn't be too hard, so I could concentrate on what the kids were doing.

With Claudia's help, we had soon designed all our squares.

"Now what?" demanded Buddy.

"Now we take another field trip." I heard a car pull into the driveway. "Perfect timing."

Vanessa tilted her head and said, "That sounds like a car. Come from afar?"

"That's right, Vanessa. Your mother has volunteered to drive us to the fabric store. She's going to take us in one of your station wagons. That way we can all go together."

Taking six kids anywhere is a major expedition. But since we are experienced baby-sitters, Claudia and I settled everybody into the station wagon (three in each seat so we could all wear seat belts) after not *too* long and headed for the fabric store downtown.

As class trips go, this one rated an A+, I could tell. The kids loved it. Vanessa trailed through the store, patting the velveteens and corduroys. Charlotte zeroed in on the embroidery thread, while Buddy fell into fascinated contemplation of the sewing machines for sale. Becca and Claudia and Haley disappeared down the aisle leading to the trim and braids.

And Nicky held his nose and said, "Euuw. It smells."

"That's the dye from the material," I told him.

I let everyone look for a little while, then shepherded them toward the remnant table in the back. "We should choose from here," I explained. "You can buy just a little bit of material, which is all you need, and you have a huge choice."

And, I added silently, we'll have enough money for it. We had asked the parents for a small fee to pay for materials.

Several people looked at us curiously as we sorted through the scraps of material, holding them up and saying things like, "Velvet would be perfect for a rose. Too bad it's blue," and "Do you think a pansy could have a face made of brown corduroy?"

Occasionally, another child would drift over and watch and once I saw someone who I think was one of Nicky's classmates peering in through the window, watching us. But we had the remnant table pretty much to ourselves.

"Remember, we can embroider things onto the pictures, too," I told everyone. "That way, Nicky, your spider can have eyes."

Nicky looked pleased. "Good. Big red eyes."

Claudia unearthed a piece of rough black wool. "This would be good for a spider, too. It's sort of fuzzy like one."

"Ick, yick," said Vanessa.

Nicky took the wool, inspected it, and added it to the pile of scraps he was making.

By the time we'd finished, we'd looked through every remnant in the store. But we had a beautiful collection of fabric.

"This is going to be the most bea-uutiful quilt," said Vanessa happily as we left the store.

I smiled down at her. "You know what, Vanessa?" I said. "You are absolutely right."

And I knew it would be — spiders and all.

CHAPTER 9

Okay, before anyone says, "Sew what?"
I just want to say that I wasn't
expecting what happened to Buddy
while I was sitting for the Barretts
on Wednesday afternoon. Call me
hopelessly naïve, (although I'd prefer
to think of it as hopelessly sophisticated and advanced) but when
Buddy Barrett came bombing through
the door with a bloody lip, the only
stitches I was thinking about were
the ones he might have to have...
fortunately, his cut wasn't as bad
as it <u>looked</u>.

wednesday

When Stacey arrived at the Barretts' house on Wednesday, she was *not* surprised when Mrs. Barrett didn't answer the door on the first ring. Or the second. Or even the third. Mrs. Barrett tends to be disorganized. So it was entirely possible that she had a) forgotten Stacey was coming; b) couldn't remember where the doorbell was; or c) both of the above. Not for one minute, though, did Stacey think that Mrs. Barrett was lying in the kitchen, say, with a broken ankle (as I would have).

And she was right not to worry. She was just about to press the bell a fourth time when the door flew open and Mrs. Barrett burst out, looking stunning as usual and as usual, trailing half-formed sentences and a bit of chaos behind her.

"Stacey!" She looked down in her purse and shouted, "Stacey's here. Buddy! Suzi! Marnie!"

Of course, Mrs. Barrett didn't have an intercom in her purse. She was looking for her keys. She pulled them out as Pow, the Barretts' basset hound, and five-year-old Suzi came tumbling out into the front hall.

"Hi, Suzi," said Stacey, smiling.

"Hi," replied Suzi. She leaned over a little, and lifted one of Pow's long, soft ears and rubbed it against her cheek. Pow wagged his tail and turned and licked Suzi's other cheek. (His ears are long enough so that he can do that.)

Stacey couldn't repress an "euwww" feeling, but since Pow and Suzi seemed happy with the arrangement, she didn't say anything.

"Did I tell you? Five-thirty, not a minute later than six, anyway — and, ah — on the notepad by the phone, the number where I, ah — " Mrs. Barrett raised her voice, "Be good, kids. Do what Stacey tells you!"

And she was gone, on an almost overwhelming tide of *Passion* perfume. Stacey interpreted what Mrs. Barrett had said to mean she'd be back by five-thirty, or at least no later than six and that on the notepad by the phone was a number where Mrs. Barrett could be reached. Mrs. Barrett hardly ever gives more instructions than that to the baby-sitters, but Stacey also knew where the list of emergency numbers was and she wasn't worried.

She closed the door behind her and bent over to pet Pow. "Where's Marnie?" she asked Suzie.

"In her room having a nap," said Suzi. "She's a *baby*."

"How about Buddy? Seen him around?"

Suzi nodded solemnly, but before she could

answer, Buddy appeared in person.

"I'm going to go out and play, okay, Stacey?"

Mrs. Barrett hadn't said anything about it and it was a nice, clear day, so Stacey said, "I don't see why not, Buddy. But you *must* stay on this block. And you can't cross the street. Understood?"

"Sure," said Buddy. " 'Bye."

Stacey smiled. "Somebody's in a hurry, huh, Suzi? Okay, now, I'm going to go check on Marnie and then why don't we open up the Kid-Kit I brought?"

Suzi's eyes lit up. "Okay!"

"I'll meet you and Pow — if he wants to join us — in the playroom."

"Come on, Pow." Suzi let go of Pow's ear. He gave her face a last lick, then trotted alongside her as she headed for the den.

Marnie was sound asleep. Stacey pulled the shade down so the sun wouldn't wake her, then returned to Suzi and Pow.

They sat down on the floor by the couch in the playroom and Suzi began to take things out of the Kid-Kit and examine them. She was reviewing the books in it and showing them to Pow ("This is *Goodnight Moon*, Pow. It's a baby book. Mommy reads it to Marnie. Oooh. This book is scary!") when the back door banged open.

Stacey jumped. Something about the force of the door slamming sounded a little ominous. And the high-speed pounding of the footsteps down the hall added to the feeling.

"Buddy? Is that you?"

"Yeah." The footsteps ran on toward the stairs.

"Hey, want to come join us?"

"No!"

With the instincts of a great baby-sitter, Stacey knew *something* was wrong. "I'll be right back," she told Suzi. Suzi nodded and pulled another book out. "You'll like this one, Pow. It's *Harry the Dirty Dog*."

Buddy was halfway up the stairs when Stacey caught up with him.

"Buddy?" He put his head down and kept going. Stacey chugged alongside him until they reached the top. Then she put her hand on his shoulder.

"Buddy?"

Buddy looked slowly up at her and she saw why he was trying to ignore her. His lip was bleeding, his T-shirt was torn, and his knees below his shorts were skinned and battered. He also looked like he was going to have a black eye before very much longer.

Keeping her voice calm and trying not to jump to any conclusions, Stacey said, "So what happened here?"

"Nothing," replied Buddy.

Stacey steered Buddy toward the bathroom. "What kind of nothing? You want to give me any details?"

Buddy shrugged. Stacey found a washcloth and washed off the scrapes, then inspected Buddy's lip. He had only a small cut, in spite of what had, at first, looked like a lot of blood.

"Here," she said. "You put the peroxide on."

"Peroxide?" Buddy's voice rose slightly.

"Or I can do it, if you want. It'll only sting a minute. Don't be afraid."

Almost ferociously, Buddy took the peroxide out of Stacey's hand. "I'm not afraid! I'm not a sissy!"

With that, he splashed a hugh amount of peroxide over his knees.

It made Stacey wince, but Buddy only scowled.

"So, give me a hint, Buddy. You met a saber-tooth tiger and didn't want to be dinner?"

Buddy continued to scowl as he shook his head.

"A rosebush leaped out from one of the flowerbeds and grabbed you and made you beg for mercy?"

"No," said Buddy shortly. "I better change shirts."

He pushed past her, but Stacey wasn't about to give up. "I'll wait outside," she said.

When Buddy didn't come out of his room, she tapped on the door. "Buddy?"

His voice was grudging. "Come in."

"Okay, Buddy, what happened?"

Buddy's face grew very red. He looked angry. "I got in a fight, okay?"

"I thought you did. I bet the other guy looks sort of like you, too."

"He sure does." Buddy made one of his hands into a fist and air-boxed for a few moments.

"How did it start?"

"He started it."

"He who?"

"I can't tell you that. I'm not a tattletale. And I'm *not* a sissy!"

"No one said you are . . . unless the guy you were fighting with did."

It was a good guess on Stacey's part. Buddy's eyes blazed. "He said taking sewing lessons is for girls and wimps and babies and sissies!"

Stacey felt a faint surge of anger. Where did kids learn to be so mean? And so sexist!

"I'd say calling someone those names is for losers," she said quietly.

Buddy shrugged. "I'm quitting."

"You're quitting? Quitting sewing lessons

with Mary Anne? Because of what someone said?"

Buddy shrugged again.

"Oh, Buddy. Just because someone says something doesn't make it true. And usually, when people tease, it's because they don't know any better. It's because they're afraid of what's different. They're the ones who are scared. They're the sissies."

Stacey stopped. She could see that what she was saying wasn't gaining any ground with Buddy. She sighed. "Okay, Buddy. I'm sorry you're quitting, and I know Mary Anne and everyone else will be, too. You'll have to call her and tell her. Meanwhile, I'd say it's time for a snack. What do you think?"

Some of the wariness left Buddy's face. "Okay," he said.

The rest of the afternoon passed uneventfully. Suzi pretended to read *Georgie's Halloween* (with a little help from Stacey) aloud to Marnie several times. Marnie didn't seem particularly scared by it despite all the thrilling sound effects Suzi added. Pow fell asleep under the sofa, with only his hind legs sticking out. Buddy lay on his stomach, pushing the pieces of a puzzle from the Kid-Kit aimlessly around.

And Mrs. Barrett arrived home late, as breathlessly as she had left. She didn't seem upset by what had happened to Buddy, especially after checking him over.

"It's too bad," she said, sighing and releasing Buddy, who had squirmed under his mother's scrutiny and took himself quickly out of reach. She walked Stacey to the door. "I wish I'd learned to sew. I was delighted Buddy was learning. Oh, well, maybe . . . well, anyway, good-bye, Stacey, and thank — "

"Good-bye," said Stacey as the door closed behind her.

Since Mrs. Barrett had returned late, the BSC meeting was over, so Stacey went home to brood over the unfairness of life.

That night after dinner, Buddy called me up.

"Buddy," I said. I hadn't seen or heard from Stacey, so I didn't have any idea why he was calling. "Hi! How are you doing?"

"I'm fine, thank you," he said stiffly. "I called to tell you I can't take sewing class anymore."

"You can't? Oh, Buddy, I'm sorry. Why?"

"I can't," he said. "Uh, I'm sorry too. I gotta go. 'Bye."

He hung up the phone before I could say anything else.

I put the receiver back slowly. It rang immediately. Weird.

"Hello?" I said.

"Hello, may I please speak to Mary Anne Spier?"

"Nicky Pike," I said. "This is Mary Anne. I recognized your voice."

Nicky said, "Oh. Well, I'm sorry, but I can't take sewing class anymore."

"You can't? Oh, Nicky, that's too bad. You know what? Buddy Barrett just called up and told me he couldn't either."

Nicky said, "He already did?"

"You knew? Nicky, what's going on?"

"Nothing," said Nicky. "We just, you know, we're busy."

I didn't want to press Nicky, since he sounded so uncomfortable, although I *was* disappointed. "Well, we'll miss you. You're good at sewing."

"Uh, thanks," said Nicky. "Well, good-bye."

"Good-bye, Nicky," I said.

No one else called to cancel, although I half expected it. I wondered what was going on, but neither Dawn nor I could come up with any logical explanations.

But we agreed: this was a topic for discussion at the next BSC meeting.

CHAPTER 10

Of course, at the next BSC meeting, I found out why Buddy had canceled his sewing lessons. No one knew who had been teasing Buddy. But we figured whoever it was probably had been teasing Nicky, too. Mal couldn't shed any more light on her brother's decision to quit, though. "He won't talk about it," she reported. "At least not now. But I think he does miss your class, Mary Anne."

I missed Buddy and Nicky, too, but the class was still going well — although it was taking us a long time to make the friendship quilt. Meanwhile, when I wasn't teaching the class, I was spending a lot of my free time at Mrs. Towne's house.

I loved taking sewing lessons with Mrs. Towne. She knew what she was talking about, and she explained things simply and clearly. Not only that, but she could always explain why things were sewn certain ways, or where a certain quilting pattern came from. Plus, she told stories about her sewing career. I liked to listen almost as much as I liked to sew. I looked forward to every lesson.

In the meantime, I tried to help her out as much as I could. I was afraid at first that our exchange wouldn't be fair — that I wouldn't be able to do enough to pay for the sewing lessons. But it wasn't that way at all. And Mrs. Towne seemed to be counting on me more and more. "You're so reliable, Mary Anne," she told me one afternoon while I was watering her flower beds. She was leaning on two canes, just inside the back door of the sun porch.

I smiled and waved. It was a soothing feeling, standing in a garden, waving the hose back and forth over the flower beds in the late afternoon sun. I had started watering the flowers every day for Mrs. Towne. I did it in the afternoons because she didn't like for them to be watered in the morning. She said some plants had a tendency to get something called "sun scald" if they had water on their leaves on a hot, sunny day.

After I watered the garden, I always went inside and watered the plants on the sunporch.

Those were a little more complicated. Not all of them needed to be watered every day, or even every other day. Some of them, like the funny, skinny pencil cactus, only needed watering when the soil grew dry. Mrs. Towne showed me how to take a pinch of soil so I could tell just how much water each plant needed, how to tell from the leaves of others whether they needed water or not.

Often, after I'd finished watering the plants, we'd have tea. I was getting very good at fixing it just right.

Which is what I'd been doing one day when I realized I was supposed to leave for a BSC meeting. I couldn't believe it! I'd almost forgotten.

I felt bad about rushing away and leaving the tea things out. Mrs. Towne said, "Don't worry, dear, I can take care of these." But that didn't make me feel any less guilty. As I dashed for Claudia's house, I resolved to work harder. I'd do twice as much the next day.

Kristy was on the phone with a client when I burst into the room.

"I'm sorry," I gasped. "I was at Mrs. Towne's and — "

Kristy signaled me to be quiet, then said, "Thank you, we'll call you back."

I grabbed the schedule book.

"The Braddocks," said Kristy. "For Saturday afternoon from one until five."

"Me, Mal, or you, Kristy," I said, checking the dates.

"Can't," said Mal. "Sorry, I forgot to tell you guys. We're going on a family outing to the mall." She rolled her eyes.

"Sure you don't need an extra baby-sitter for that?" teased Stacey.

"Uh-uh," said Jessi, grinning. "I'm going, too. We're getting paid in ice cream after it's over."

"Why don't you take the job, Mary Anne?" asked Kristy. I knew she was, in her own Kristy way, trying to make up for the mean "You're late" look she'd given when I'd burst in.

I smiled to show I understood, but I shook my head. "I can't. Thanks, though. Can't you do it, Kristy?"

"Sure. But why can't you?" asked Kristy as I wrote her name in the book.

"I need to be free to help Mrs. Towne. In fact, I probably shouldn't schedule any baby-sitting jobs for awhile. At least until she's back on her feet."

"I thought she was back on her feet. Isn't it just a broken ankle? She's on crutches, right?" Kristy is nothing if not direct.

"Crutches or her canes. She's getting better with them," I said.

"And doesn't a nurse come every day, too?"

Oh my lord. Kristy was turning into a pros- ecutor, like those lawyers on TV.

"The nurse is for physical therapy. Besides, I'm paying for my sewing lessons by helping Mrs. Towne out," I reminded Kristy.

Dawn said, "It seems like you're putting in an awful lot of time and work at Mrs. Towne's, Mary Anne."

Before I could answer, Stacey said, "And if you're giving up baby-sitting jobs it's like you're paying twice."

Part of me wanted to argue. Part of me was hurt that they hadn't realized they were seeing the new, unselfish me. And part of me thought, They'll never understand.

Fortunately, the phone rang again, and we got busy. By the time the client rush was over, we'd moved on to other topics.

When I reached Mrs. Towne's house the next day, I decided that what her kitchen floor needed was a good mopping. I settled Mrs. Towne in her sewing room, then found the mop and bucket. I unhooked the apron from the back of the pantry door, noticing as I did how beautifully made the apron was. No store-bought apron here, but one with a bib and a loop on the side for a towel, and a big patch pocket with embroidered edging.

It was a little big, but not much. I filled the

bucket, picked up the mop, turned, and somehow managed to knock the bottle of Murphy's oil soap over. I made a grab for it, snagged it, stepped in the bucket of water I'd filled and turned the whole thing over. I just saved myself from falling by grabbing a chair.

What a mess!

Oh, well. At least I hadn't dropped the soap.

"Are you okay?" called Mrs. Towne. I guess the metal bucket had made a lot of racket.

"Fine," I called back reassuringly. "No problem."

"Mary Anne?" said a familiar voice from the front door.

"Dawn?" I said. I gave my foot a shake. The bucket stuck to it. No way was I stuck in the bucket. Was I?

"Can we come in? It's me and the Arnolds."

I'd forgotten that Dawn was sitting for the Arnolds that day, and that she'd said she might stop by.

"Uh, sure, come on back." I gave my foot another shake and the bucket came off and clattered across the floor. My feet were soaked, and I was standing in a gloppy pool of soap and water.

Carolyn and Marilyn appeared at the door, took one look at the puddle of water and shrieked, "Goody!"

Two seconds later, the twins were sliding in the water on the floor as if it were a skating rink.

"Wait a minute, wait a minute!" I cried, while Dawn made a grab for the nearest twin.

"What happened here?" asked Dawn. I looked at the floor, I looked at my feet, and I looked at the girls' faces.

"It's a long story," I said, and burst out laughing.

It took awhile to clean up the kitchen. I tried to use the water to mop the floor by just adding the Murphy's oil soap, but it wasn't easy. I didn't want to add too much soap, because I knew that with all that water I'd just create more soap suds. And more soap. And *more* soap.

By the time I'd finished that, Dawn and the twins had had a visit with Mrs. Towne and were on their way out.

"I'm walking Carolyn and Marilyn back home," Dawn said. "Want to join us and then maybe go get a soda or something?"

"I can't," I replied. "I still have to water the plants and the garden. Oh, and the laundry. I almost forgot about the laundry."

"Are you sure?" said Dawn.

"Thanks, but I'll catch up with you later."

"Okay . . ." The three of them trailed away. I returned to my chores.

As I was heading home, I looked at my watch. I'd wanted to call Claudia and work with her on the design of the quilt for my sewing class. We had the materials and we were making progress, but Claudia had such a good eye for color and texture that I'd hoped she and I could go back to the fabric shop for some extras.

Now I was too late. As it was, I barely got home in time for dinner. And afterward, I was just plain tired.

Dawn stuck her head in the door as I lay sprawled across the bed, staring at the ceiling. "You look beat," she said.

"Ummm."

"Well, I guess I'll come back later."

I laughed. "Later, I'll be asleep." I couldn't help myself. I yawned.

Smiling, Dawn gave me a little wave. "You'll be asleep in the next five minutes, I'd say. Talk to you later."

"Okay," I said. "It's not important is it?"

But Dawn had all ready gone.

She was right. I fell asleep about five minutes later.

The next morning after breakfast, I sat down on the back steps and just stared at nothing. It felt good. I stretched. A hammock had been hung in the backyard. Mostly my father stretched out in it when he had a chance. I'd never understood its appeal before, but I thought I might give it a try. I lowered myself into it.

Hmm. Not bad. Not a bad way at all to spend a peaceful summer morning. . . .

"Mary Anne! Mary Anne!"

I sat up. Sharon was standing at the back door, waving. "Telephone. It's Mrs. Towne."

Mrs. Towne. Oh, no! Had she had another accident?

I flew out of the hammock and ran to the phone.

"Hello," I gasped.

"Mary Anne. You sound out of breath. Is this a bad time to call?"

"No! Not at all. Is anything wrong?"

"Not a thing — except this ankle of mine. I was just wondering . . . I have some sewing supplies upstairs in my bedroom. I can't quite manage the stairs, as you know, and I need some fabric for one of the projects I'm working on. Could you possibly come over when you have a moment and get a few things down for me?"

"Sure. No problem. I'll be there right away." I hung up the phone and turned to find Dawn behind me.

"Mrs. Towne?" she asked.

"Yes, but don't worry. It's not an emergency," I told her.

"Are you going to be gone long?"

"I don't know . . ." I said. Inside, I sighed. Part of me (the lazy, inconsiderate part, no doubt) wished I were still lying in that hammock. I pushed the thought aside and headed for Mrs. Towne's house.

I didn't see Dawn again until that afternoon. She waved at me from the Kishis' car as I was coming home, all grungy from yard work at Mrs. Towne's. (Weeds have a way of creeping up on flower beds, I guess.) Dawn was in the car with Stacey and Claudia. I found out when I got home that they'd left for the mall.

For a moment I was hurt that they'd gone without me. But then I realized that I couldn't very well expect them to plan their schedules around mine.

It was no big deal, I told myself. Besides, I needed a shower.

The shower felt great, and I felt better, too. And when Logan called, I realized how long it had been since I'd seen him.

Especially when he said, "Hello, stranger."

"Logan? How are you doing?"

"In the years that have passed since I saw you last — "

"Uh-oh, a poet," I said. "Have you been hanging around with Vanessa Pike?"

" — I have aged. But if you'll go out with

me soon, like tomorrow maybe, my condition will improve."

"I can't tomorrow," I said. "I have to do some stuff for Mrs. Towne."

"The next day?"

"That's not good either."

"Mary Anne! Are you trying to tell me something?"

"Only that I'm really, really busy, Logan." I sighed. How had life gotten so complicated? "Listen, what about Friday? We'll spend the whole day together. We'll go on a picnic, take a bike ride . . ."

"Decent!" said Logan.

Had I just been thinking about how complicated life was? Wrong. It was wonderful. I was going to spend all of Friday with Logan.

"I can hardly wait," Logan told me.

I wondered if he could feel how big my smile was over the phone as I replied, "Me neither. I can hardly wait either."

CHAPTER 11

Dawn stuck her head in the door of my room.

"Logan's here," she said.

I glanced at the clock on my dresser. Eleven A.M. sharp. I took one last look in the mirror and headed downstairs.

Logan was at the kitchen table drinking Orangina with Dawn.

"Hey," he said in that soft drawl that always made me feel good. Today, it made me feel *extra* good. I hadn't seen Logan in forever, and now I had the whole day ahead of me to spend with him doing everything and anything — except housework.

"So what's the plan?" asked Dawn, pouring out some Orangina for me.

"Thanks, Dawn. What a *wonderful* day! Isn't it a wonderful day?"

Logan gave me a significant look and said, "It sure is."

I blushed a little, but I smiled to let him know I agreed.

And Dawn went on, "It *is* definitely a decent day. I'd say some serious porch-sitting activity is required. Let's go sit out there."

Dawn led the way to the porch and sat down on the top step. Logan sat next to her and I slid past them and sat on the step below and leaned back against Logan.

"You never answered my question," Dawn pointed out. "What's the deal for the day, guys? Hanging out? Major activity? Variations on the porch-sitting theme?"

Logan laughed. "Wellll — it was hard deciding, wouldn't you say, Mary Anne?"

I nodded. "We finally decided we'd ride our bikes to the lake and spend the whole day swimming and hiking and having a picnic lunch."

"Excellent choice," said Dawn. "The sun at the lake should be a killer this time of year."

Just then, as if the word killer were his cue, Tigger came leaping out from under the steps, taking wild swipes at a monarch butterfly. The butterfly didn't seem to notice it was being chased. It kept making lovely zig-zag flight patterns across the lawn, gradually flying higher and higher. That didn't stop Tigger, though. He persisted, twisting and twirling in the air until the butterfly made a sudden loop and disappeared into the branches of a tree.

We all burst out laughing. Tigger, in true cat fashion, pretended he didn't notice. He turned his back on us, sat down, and began furiously washing his paw and face.

We hung out on the steps for awhile longer, watching Tigger and talking. Then Logan and I went inside and began packing our picnic lunch.

"I'm not helping you with this," said Dawn. "I *know* what the word picnic really stands for, you guys: junk food extravaganza."

Logan pretended to be hurt. "Junk food? Junk food? Potato chips are an important source of . . . of . . ."

"Potato vitamins," I supplied.

"Uh-huh," said Dawn. "I forgot. The potato chip vitamin. Sort of like vitamin C, right?"

"Right," agreed Logan. "You need some every day!"

We didn't pack just potato chips, though (although we included plenty). Logan had brought some homemade pimento cheese from his house. (That's cheese and mayonnaise and pimentoes all mixed together. I hadn't heard of it until I met Logan, but he says he practically grew up eating pimento cheese sandwiches in the south.) I made cream cheese and jelly sandwiches on brown bread, and snagged some salsa to go with the chips.

Salsa made me think of avocados, so I made some avocado and cheese sandwiches, too. Then Logan "invented" an avocado and pimento cheese sandwich.

"I think that about covers it," he said.

"Wait," I answered. I dug around in the refrigerator and pulled out a bunch of grapes, then found a package of double fudge Oreos where I'd secretly stashed them in the pantry.

"*Out*-standing," said Logan. We loaded the picnic into our knapsacks on top of the swimming stuff and headed out the door. We were wheeling our bikes down the drive when I heard Dawn calling me.

"Mary Anne! Mary Anne!"

I turned and shaded my eyes so I could see her on the porch. "What is it?"

"It's Mrs. Towne," said Dawn. "She says she needs your help."

"Just a minute," I told Logan, taking off my backpack and setting it on the ground. I ran as fast as I could back into the house and picked up the telephone.

"Mary Anne? Oh, good. I was so worried you wouldn't be there."

"Mrs. Towne! What's wrong?"

"Oh, dear, I didn't mean to worry you. It's just that I need some things that are on the top shelf of a closet and I can't reach them. And — I know this is going to sound silly, but — a wasp has gotten into the kitchen and I can't seem to shoo it out." She gave a little laugh. "Wasps make me, well, *nervous*."

"Me, too," I said. Poor Mrs. Towne. "I'll come right over."

But when I hung up the phone, I found Dawn standing there.

"I have to go over to Mrs. Towne's," I said.

"Oh," said Dawn. That's all she said. Just "oh." But something about the way she said it made me answer, "Well, how would you like to be old and helpless and all alone?"

"I'm not into helpless," said Dawn, and left before I could answer.

I remembered Logan then, and hurried back outside where he was waiting patiently.

"Mrs. Towne needs me to come over right away," I said.

Logan wasn't as neutral as Mary Anne. "Now?" he said. "You're kidding!"

"No!"

"An emergency?" asked Logan.

"Not exactly," I replied. I explained what Mrs. Towne wanted. "How could I say no?" I concluded. "It would have been selfish. And Mrs. Towne needs help."

Logan shook his head. "I guess."

"C'mon, Logan. We'll go over to Mrs. Towne's house and help her out and then we'll have our picnic."

"It's afternoon already," Logan pointed out. But he was turning his bicycle in the direction of Mrs. Towne's house even as he was speaking.

"Thanks, Logan," I said gratefully.

Mrs. Towne met us at the door of her house. I introduced Logan to her and he shook hands with Mrs. Towne. Mrs. Towne told me which closet she had been talking about and what she needed out of it. Then Logan and Mrs. Towne made their way slowly down the hall toward the kitchen. I hoped Logan would see how nice Mrs. Towne was. I wanted him to like her.

When I returned from the closet, Mrs. Towne was standing by the door that led from the hall into the kitchen. The door was closed.

"It's in there," she said, almost whispering.

"Don't worry," said Logan. He pretended to flex his muscles. "We'll get the varmint."

"We won't kill it, though, okay, Logan?" I said.

"Whatever you say," he answered.

We pushed the kitchen door open and slipped inside. Mrs. Towne closed it firmly behind us.

The wasp was easy to spot. It was buzzing against the kitchen window angrily.

It wasn't so easy to catch.

First we tried to put a glass over it. Once we'd trapped it against the window with the glass, we could slide a piece of cardboard or something under the glass and just take it outside.

But the wasp refused to go along with our plan.

"Here, let me try," said Logan, after I'd missed the wasp about a zillion times.

I climbed carefully down from the kitchen sink and handed the glass to Logan. He crouched down, lifted the glass — and fell backward. "Arrgh!"

The wasp sailed out into the kitchen over our heads as I caught Logan to keep him from falling. I staggered under the weight of him while he scrambled to try and get his feet out of the sink and onto the floor.

It almost worked. Except that Logan tripped over the edge of the sink. The next thing I knew, we'd landed with a crash in the middle of the kitchen floor.

"Are you okay?" Mrs. Towne called anxiously from the other side of the door.

"Terrific," said Logan.

"We're fine, Mrs. Towne," I answered. "Don't worry."

"I think I'm injured," said Logan. "I think I need someone to kiss me and make me feel better."

He leaned toward me — and the wasp dive bombed us!

"Eeek," I screamed, scooting backward.

"Aaah!" croaked Logan, doing the same thing.

The wasp rose up and made a triumphant circle of the kitchen ceiling.

"Where's the broom?" asked Logan.

"No!" I said. "You can't kill it."

"Why not? It's trying to kill us!"

"It doesn't know we're trying to help it," I said.

We sat for a minute watching the wasp circle. Every third or fourth circle, it came back to bang on the kitchen window.

Suddenly I had an idea. "What if we just raised the window and took the screen out? Then the wasp could fly out the window and away."

"*Great* idea, Mary Anne." Logan got up and held out his hand to me. "You stand in the sink this time. I think it would be safer."

He hoisted me up to the sink and I raised the window. The screen lifted easily. I climbed safely to the floor and we settled down to watch the wasp. Sure enough, on the fifth circle it flew to the window. It didn't even slow down. It just sailed on through.

"Here's to a job well done," said Logan, leaning over to give me a kiss.

The kitchen door opened and Mrs. Towne said, "Did you get it?"

Trying not to look as if she'd surprised us, I said, "We sure did. We opened the kitchen window and it flew right out."

"Oh, good," said Mrs. Towne. "Now, why don't you let me fix you some lunch, to thank you for all this."

"Oh, no, that's okay," I began, but she waved her hand. "No, I insist. It's past lunchtime anyway. You must be hungry. I am!"

"Well . . ."

"We have this picnic lunch packed," said Logan.

"Picnic lunch? Why don't I make a few more things to add to it, and you can eat your picnic on the sunporch with me. It's a lovely day for it. Do say yes, Mary Anne. I feel so bad about calling you in the middle of the day to do this for me."

"Well," I said. I didn't want to be rude. And I was hungry. The picnic would taste as good on the porch as at the lake. Wouldn't it?

I looked at Logan. He looked at me.

"Thank you," he said. "We'd enjoy a picnic lunch on the porch."

Mrs. Towne beamed. "I'm delighted. Now, let's get everything set up . . ."

It *was* a nice picnic lunch. Mrs. Towne recognized the pimento cheese right away and she and Logan had a long talk about the merits of pimento cheese sandwiches versus regular cheese sandwiches.

After lunch, Mrs. Towne fixed tea for us to drink with the cookies and grapes.

"That was delicious," she said when we'd finished.

"It sure was," I agreed.

"Let us help you clean up," said Logan, jumping to his feet. He didn't give the impression he was hurrying, but in almost no time we'd cleared the dishes, washed them, and put them away.

I took the hint. And it was growing late.

"We have to go," I told Mrs. Towne.

To my relief, she nodded. "Yes, it is getting on in the day, isn't it? Well, I'm so glad I got to meet you, Logan. Do come by again."

"Thank you," said Logan. He didn't say anything else as Mrs. Towne hobbled with us to the door and waved good-bye while we walked our bicycles down the bumpy driveway.

I could tell Logan was not happy.

"Okay, what is it?" I said, although I had an idea I knew.

I was right.

Logan took a deep breath and shook his head. Then he said, "Mrs. Towne is a nice woman, don't get me wrong. And I'm glad

116

we could help her. But this isn't exactly the way I had planned to spend today, you know?"

"I know, Logan. Me, neither. But what else could we have done?"

Logan shook his head again. He didn't answer.

"Why don't we ride over to the park?" I suggested. "There's a pond there and we can just hang out. It's not the same as the lake but . . ."

Logan nodded. "Okay," he said.

And that's what we did until it was time for me to go to the BSC meeting.

That night, I was tired. Not just my body — my brain. My thoughts kept going around and around like the wasp in the kitchen.

I'd wanted too much to be a better person, someone not so selfish and self-centered. Helping Mrs. Towne out seemed to be a part of that. Wouldn't refusing to help her — to go off and have fun at the lake — be *truly*, totally selfish? It made me feel awful, but I kept wishing I'd pretended I hadn't heard Dawn when she'd called me back to the phone that morning.

And, on the other hand, maybe it was selfish of me not to think of Logan's needs, too. We'd barely seen each other lately. I'd promised him we'd spend the whole day together.

And we'd ended up spending most of it at Mrs. Towne's.

That had made Logan feel bad. And it made me feel worse, because I knew I'd let him down. But why couldn't he understand about Mrs. Towne?

I didn't know what to do. What was the right thing? Weren't the needs of a lonely old woman more important than Logan's?

My head hurt from thinking and thinking and thinking when I finally fell asleep. And I still hadn't come up with an answer.

CHAPTER 12

When you have four brothers, you think you've seen all the weird things male siblings can come up with. But Nicky surprised me, I admit it.

Hey, Mal, I wasn't surprised. I'd figured out what was happening! I just didn't think Nicky would take it so far....

Sure, Jessi. That was why you kept trying to convince Nicky that real men don't have to wear tool belts...

As Mal and Jessi were heading from the library toward Slate Street that afternoon, where they were about to start a baby-sitting job with Mal's seven brothers and sisters, they talked about the books they'd checked out. Mal had found one by Louise Fitzhugh called *Nobody's Family Is Going to Change*. Jessi had talked her into it. She liked the story of a boy who wanted to be a dancer like his uncle, only the boy's rigid, uptight father wouldn't let him, because he says boys don't dance. Jessi said it was a really excellent book, and Mallory was willing to give her the benefit of the doubt, since Louise Fitzhugh had also written *Harriet the Spy*, which both Mal and Jessi happened to like a lot.

As it turned out, the book was a sort of foreshadowing to the afternoon.

Of course, they didn't know it when they arrived at the Pikes'. "I'm going to play tennis until I drop," Mrs. Pike told them. She gathered up her tennis gear and added, "Adam and Jordan are watching horror movies in the rec room, Vanessa is sewing in her room. Byron, Margo, and Claire are building a maze for Frodo in Byron's room (Frodo is the Pikes' hamster). And Nicky is," she picked up her keys and gave them a little jingle for emphasis, "weirdly energetic."

"Have a good time, Mom," said Mal as her mother headed out to the station wagon. Mrs. Pike waved over her shoulder, and Mal and Jessi settled in for an afternoon of baby-sitting. They dumped the library books and their packs in Mal's room and then decided to check on the kids.

Sure enough, they found Adam and Jordan watching an old Boris Karloff movie. "Check this out," said Adam, looking over his shoulder as Mal and Jessi came in. "He's a mummy, see? And he's about to walk!"

One look at the screen was enough to convince both Mal and Jessi that it was *not* something they wanted to check out.

"Um, thanks, guys," said Mal. "When you're done, maybe we'll have a snack or something."

"Okay," said Jordan, "but you're missing a great movie!"

Unconvinced, Mal and Jessi headed upstairs. Byron (who is a little more sensitive than his two brothers, proving that although they are triplets, they are not entirely identical) had opted out of the horror movie to work on an elaborate maze on the floor of his room.

Claire, who is five, jumped up when she saw them and ran to throw her arms around Jessi. "Helllooooo," she sang out.

"Oof," said Jessi. "Hi, Claire. Hi, Margo. Hi, Byron."

"Umm," said Byron, frowning with concentration as he propped a paper towel tube against the open door of Frodo's hamster cage. Frodo didn't seem interested. He burrowed into the cedar chips that lined the bottom of the cage.

The maze consisted of plastic fences from a bucket of farm toys, stacks of books, and a shoebox with a hole at each end. More books and another tube had been pushed to one side of the maze, like leftover materials at a construction site.

"Frodo," said Byron. "Come out, Frodo."

"Here, Frodo," coaxed Margo.

Frodo ignored them.

"It's a maze," explained Claire.

"Amazing," said Jessi.

That earned a brief, quick grin from Byron and a giggle from Margo. Claire, looking a little puzzled, giggled too.

"Can we have a snack now?" asked Claire.

"Not *right* this minute," said Jessi. "Maybe in a little while. Besides, you have to finish your maze."

"Okay," said Claire. She released her stranglehold on Jessi's waist and skipped back to the maze.

"Frodo," coaxed Byron.

Frodo continued to ignore them all.

Shaking her head and smiling, Mal said, "Keep the door closed so he doesn't get out of the room, okay?"

"Okay," said Margo.

"Let's check on Vanessa and Nicky and then maybe make some Tollhouse cookies," suggested Mal. "I'm starving."

"Me, too," said Jessi.

Vanessa was in her room, bent over a square of green, sewing with intense concentration. She didn't even look up when Jessi said, "How's it going?"

"I'm working on daisies, now," answered Vanessa.

"Well, if you get hungry, Mal and I thought we'd make some cookies."

That brought Vanessa's head up. "Can I come sit in the kitchen?"

"You want to help?" asked Mal. The power of cookies, she was thinking.

But Vanessa shook her head. "No, thanks. But I can talk to you while I work on my quilt blocks. Sort of like a quilting bee. You see?"

"Sounds fine," said Mal. "By the way, have you seen Nicky?"

Vanessa shrugged. "I just have to finish this petal," she answered.

Correctly figuring out Vanessa's response, Mal told Jessi, "Well, I'll check around for him and meet you in the kitchen."

A few minutes later, as Jessi was getting out the ingredients for cookies, Vanessa entered the kitchen carrying her shoebox sewing kit. Setting it carefully on the table, she sat down, opened the box, took out a needle and thread, threaded the needle, put the thread back in the box, took out the green quilt block, and bent her head back over her quilting.

Jessi had stopped to watch, impressed and a little amused by Vanessa's intensity. Vanessa didn't notice. She didn't even look up when Mal came back into the kitchen.

"So far, no Nicky," reported Mal. "I'm going to check the — "

Before Mal could say what she was going to check, the front door slammed open.

"Don't move," a voice ordered. "I've got you in my sights."

It was Nicky. He was dressed in green — khaki cut-offs, a lime green T-shirt, kelly green socks, and what looked like his father's work boots. Around his waist hung a tool belt holding about a million different tools. He was waving a toy gun.

"Nicky?" said Mal, surprised.

"I'm a mighty hunter," announced Nicky. He saw what Vanessa was doing and narrowed his eyes. "A *hunter*, strong and brave and true!"

"Is that why you're dressed in green? Are you Robin Hood?" asked Jessi.

"No! This is camouflage," said Nicky. "I blend in with the woods. I can sneak up on my prey."

"Oh," said Mal.

Vanessa was more outspoken. She glanced up, then looked back down at her sewing, saying, "You wouldn't blend in at all."

Nicky narrowed his eyes into a real scowl. "How would you know? You're just a girl."

"You're just a boy," countered Vanessa. She held up her square of the quilt. "Just a boy," she repeated.

"Well, I'm not sewing a dumb old quilt, like a *girl*," said Nicky. With his free hand he reached down to the tool belt and came up with a tape measure. "I build things!"

Vanessa shifted her attention from the quilt square to the tape measure for a moment. "You use tape measures to sew, the same as you use them to build things."

Realizing that he was holding a tape measure, Nicky hastily stuffed it into the pocket of his shorts. "Aw, you know what I mean. It's not the same thing!"

"Why not?" asked Vanessa. "I'm building a quilt out of blocks, except they're blocks of material." She tilted her head, obviously admiring the square on which she was working.

Nicky scowled. "That's not the same," he repeated. He folded his arms and waited. No one said anything.

Finally, Jessi said, "We're making some chocolate chip cookies. Also . . ." (she held up another bag that was half full of coconut) ". . . some chocolate chip coconut cookies. Want to help?"

This was the wrong thing to say to Nicky the Macho Man. "No!" shouted Nicky.

"Well, Byron and Claire and Margo are building a maze up in Byron's room for Frodo," said Jessi. "Maybe they'd let you join them."

Nicky kept his arms folded and his scowl in place.

"No, huh? How about horror movies with Adam and Jordan?" asked Mal.

Nicky wavered on that one, until Vanessa said, "They're not even scary horror movies. They're funny."

Uh-oh. Not tough enough for Nicky. He shook his head.

"Well, what do you want to do?"

"Build a fort," said Nicky. "We could play war."

"No one wants to play war, Nicky," Vanessa told him calmly.

126

Nicky scowled again. Then he said, "May I call Buddy and ask him to come over?"

"I don't see why not," replied Mal.

Still scowling (although not as ferociously), Nicky charged out of the kitchen, his tool belt clanking.

Jessi and Mal exchanged looks over Vanessa's head.

But they didn't say anything. Instead, Mal opened a cabinet, studied it thoughtfully, and said, "What about some peanut butter cookies, too?"

"Mal! We're going to have a *ton* of cookies!"

"That's okay, Jessi. We've got a ton of kids here. Besides, we can save some."

"Then let's really be creative." Jessi joined Mal in her perusal of the cabinet. "What else is in there?"

"Frodo is a silly-billy-goo-goo," a voice announced.

"Silly," another voice agreed.

Claire and Margo came into the kitchen, followed by Byron. The girls plopped down at the kitchen table.

"Couldn't get him to do the maze, huh?" asked Jessi sympathetically.

Byron said, "It might have been too complicated. What kind of cookies are you making?"

"So far, chocolate chip, coconut chocolate chip, peanut butter . . ."

"Peanut butter chocolate chip," suggested Vanessa.

"That too," agreed Jessi.

"Decent," said Byron. "Can I watch?"

"Why don't you help?" asked Mal.

"Me, too," said Claire.

"Me, too," echoed Margo.

"Pretend you're a baker," Jessi said.

"We'll be the Pike-Ramsey Bakery, cookies a specialty," said Mal.

In short order, she and Jessi had everyone (except Vanessa, who needed to concentrate on her daisy) in aprons, assigned to various tasks. And the roster of cookies was growing. At Byron's suggestion, they'd branched out into oatmeal.

Just then, the doorbell rang. "I'll get it," shouted Nicky, his feet thundering down the hall. A moment later two sets of feet thundered back. Buddy Barrett stuck his head in the door.

"Hi," he said.

"Hi, Buddy," said Jessi. "Want to help us make cookies?"

"No," said Nicky.

"What kind?" asked Buddy.

"Chocolate chip, coconut chocolate chip,

peanut butter, peanut butter chocolate chip, and oatmeal," replied Mal.

"What about M & M's? Could we make some cookies with those?"

"Sure," said Mal.

"Cool," said Buddy. He rooted around in his backpack and came up with a large, half-empty, squashed-looking bag of M & M's.

"Buddy! We're playing fort," said Nicky, looking outraged. "You should come, too, Byron."

"Why?" asked Byron.

"Because making cookies is . . ." (Nicky hesitated, obviously having second thoughts about calling Byron a sissy) ". . . is for girls."

Byron looked at his brother and made a face. "Says who?" answered Byron.

Seeming to take courage from Byron's attitude, Buddy came into the kitchen and put the M & M's on the table. He looked at Vanessa's daisy quilt block. "It's pretty," he said.

"Thank you," replied Vanessa.

"Buddy!" said Nicky.

Buddy looked guiltily over his shoulder. "Okay," he replied. To the kitchen at large he said, "You can keep the M & M's."

"We'll make them, we'll bake them, we'll shake them into cookies," sang Vanessa.

Soon the oven was full of cookies, with more

stacked around the counters waiting to go in as soon as the first batch was done, while the bakers added more fillings to more dough and rolled it out to cut into cookies. The smell of baking cookies filled the kitchen.

It was hardly surprising that, a few minutes later, Adam and Jordan joined the bakers too.

"What happened to the mummy?" asked Jessi.

Adam grabbed his throat and made rasping sounds.

"I see," said Jessi. "Well, find an apron and make some cookies."

"Okay," agreed Adam. He and Jordan were soon creating their own flavors of cookies with the ingredients Jessi and Mal had set out, which now included raisins and peanuts.

While Mal pulled the first trays of cookies out, and Jessi poured the milk, a mad scramble, Pike-style, broke out for chairs around the kitchen table. Although Jessi is used to the exuberance of the Pikes, she still half expected chairs to crash over and maybe the table to collapse, but everyone got a seat unscathed. And of course, Vanessa kept sewing through it all.

"I'll go tell Nicky and Buddy the cookies are ready," said Mal.

Apparently, eating cookies was not on Nicky's list of sissy activities, because a few minutes later he and Buddy followed Mal into the kitchen and claimed places at one end of the table. Buddy was now wearing an old leather belt with a hammer and a screwdriver precariously hooked on it. Nicky had added a cap to his outfit, and had stuck branches and leaves under it.

Jordan raised his eyebrows. "Nicky, you look weird. Like a tree."

Nicky had just stuffed a cookie in his mouth. His face grew red as he chewed, trying to finish it in a hurry so he could answer. At last he said, "Well, what about what you're wearing? Huh?"

Jordan looked down at his T-shirt, shorts, and apron. "What about it?"

"An apron! You're wearing an apron!"

"Yeah," said Jordan. "So?"

"Aprons are for *girls*."

Jordan looked at Adam. Adam looked at Byron. Then the triplets all looked at Nicky and burst out laughing.

Nicky's face grew even redder. "Stop laughing!"

Of course, that made his brothers laugh even harder.

Enraged, Nicky jumped up and charged out of the kitchen. "Come on, Buddy!"

Buddy obeyed, but not before he'd grabbed a big handful of cookies.

"Thanks," he remembered to say, as he hurried after Nicky.

The timer for the second batch of cookies rang, and the triplets stopped laughing to attend to the more important business at hand.

The Pike-Ramsey Bakery made about six dozen cookies, and after extensive taste tests conducted on chocolate chip, raisin chocolate chip, oatmeal chocolate chip, M & M cookies, peanut peanut butter cookies, peanut butter coconut cookies, and a few other varieties, voted chocolate chip cookies their favorite.

Nicky and Buddy didn't vote. They stayed in the backyard the rest of the afternoon, looking hotter and more miserable the more furiously they hammered away at their fort.

They reminded Jessi of a saying on a poster she'd seen: "Suppose they had a war and nobody came." Because some kid had teased him, Nicky had declared war on what he thought was sissy stuff. Now he was discovering how much stuff that meant he couldn't do. He was having a war, and it just wasn't any fun.

CHAPTER 13

"And he was wearing this tool belt," said Mallory, shaking her head.

"Nicky Pike, Macho Man." Jessi cracked up all over again.

I was at a meeting of the BSC and I was having a great time, like being at a party, almost. I'd been so busy lately that I hadn't even *seen* Jessi or Mal or Claudia or Stacey or Kristy — not to mention Dawn — in what felt like forever.

"I don't think Nicky has quite gotten the idea that being a macho man means there's more stuff he can't do, than stuff he can do," said Stacey.

"Yeah. I hope he gets it soon." Mal rolled her eyes. "Otherwise I expect him to start pounding on his chest, like some gorilla. Although," she added thoughtfully, "between the triplets and Vanessa, he's not getting away with much."

"Poor Nicky," said Dawn.

"Hey," said Kristy. "Being a male chauvinist pig — or even a male chauvinist piglet — doesn't earn any sympathy from me!"

"Tough Kristy," teased Claudia. "Have some Gummi worms."

"Thanks," said Kristy. She chewed for a moment, then said, "Somehow, they taste better than those cookies you brought, Mal. No offense."

Mal laughed. "That was the last batch — I don't know what kind you'd call them. We put everything that was left over in the batter."

"That explains it," said Kristy.

The phone rang and Kristy answered it crisply, in spite of the Gummi worms (that's Kristy for you). "Baby-sitters Club."

She listened a moment, then motioned to me. "It's for you."

It was Mrs. Towne.

I took the phone from Kristy, listened to Mrs. Towne, and said, "Of course I can. I'll be there right away."

I hung up and looked around. It felt as if I'd just arrived at the meeting. But I was glad I'd thought to give Mrs. Towne Claudia's number, so she'd know where to reach me during club meetings.

"Is it an emergency?" asked Kristy, frowning. I could see that, as club president, her sense of organization was offended because I was leaving early.

"I'm sure it is," I replied.

"Well, okay," said Kristy. The phone rang again, and while Kristy was taking down the information, I slid the appointment book over to Dawn, waved at everyone, grabbed my backpack, and hurried out.

It wasn't an emergency after all. Mrs. Towne just needed me to bring up a box from the basement.

"Just set it on the kitchen table. Thank you so much, Mary Anne. I know I'm technically able to navigate stairs now that I'm off the crutches, but I'm still a little leery of them."

"I can understand that," I answered. "But I'm glad this wasn't an emergency."

"An emergency? Oh, no. What gave you that idea? I hope you didn't worry . . ."

"It's okay. . . . Well, I'd better be getting home."

"You wouldn't like to stay for a late tea with cookies?"

"Thanks, Mrs. Towne. But it's almost dinnertime. And I ate a ton of cookies at our meeting."

"Well," said Mrs. Towne, "if you're sure. Thanks again." We walked slowly back down the hall and I went outside and got on my bicycle. I glanced back as I rode out of the driveway. Mrs. Towne was standing in the doorway, looking so lonely.

I waved. She waved back and closed the door, and I headed home, feeling tired, annoyed — and guilty.

At the next BSC meeting, I told Mal how much I liked the cookies she'd made with everything in them. (She'd brought more to the meeting.)

"Wait'll I tell the triplets," answered Mal. "They'll love it."

"Maybe you should reconsider it, Mal," Jessi said. "They might want to make the same cookies again."

Mal looked thoughtful and we all burst out laughing.

"I thought they tasted pretty good." Claudia looked around, only half kidding. That made us all laugh even harder.

And that's when the phone rang.

I knew who it was the moment Kristy nodded, looking at me. I reached out and took the receiver.

It was Mrs. Towne. She wondered if I could come over.

"Is it an emergency?" I asked.

"Well, no," she said. She sounded surprised — and a little hurt.

136

I felt bad. What could I do?

"Okay," I said. "I'll be over as soon as possible."

I hung up the phone, feeling six pairs of eyes on me.

"Mrs. Towne," I explained, unnecessarily. "I better go."

"*Is* it an emergency?" asked Kristy.

"Well, no," I said. "Listen, I have to leave. I'll talk to you guys later."

I'd been edging toward the door while I was talking. Before Kristy could say anything else, I whisked out and dashed down the stairs, feeling guilty. Again.

Guilty. And angry. Angry that I'd had to leave the second BSC meeting in a row for something that wasn't an emergency. Angry that Kristy was obviously annoyed with me. Angry that I'd had to defend myself just for being nice.

Nice.

Nice.

The word repeated itself in my head as I pedaled my bicycle. And the more it repeated itself, the more I didn't like the sound of it.

Nice isn't always good. Or unselfish. Or the right thing to do. Sometimes, it's just the easiest thing to do.

I was going to have to do something not so

nice now, I decided, as I reached Mrs. Towne's house. I was going to have to talk to her about our relationship.

After all, her ankle was healing nicely. She could go up and down stairs now. She only needed one cane for getting around. And her original bulky cast had been changed to a lightweight walking one. She was a little slower, maybe, but almost as mobile as before her accident.

"Mary Anne." Mrs. Towne met me at the door, a smile of welcome on her face. I felt a horrible pang of guilt shoot through me. How could I do anything to hurt Mrs. Towne's feelings?

But I had to.

I took a deep breath. "Mrs. Towne. Hi. Listen, could we talk?"

The welcoming smile on Mrs. Towne's face faded a little. But she stepped back and motioned me in. "Of course. Come on in. Why don't we sit on the sunporch. Would you like some tea?"

"No. No, thank you. Not right now."

"You're sure?"

"Yes," I said. "I'm sure."

When we'd taken our places at the table, Mrs. Towne said, "Is something wrong, Mary Anne?"

"No," I said. "Not exactly. Well . . ." I drew

in a deep breath. "Yes. Yes, there is. Mrs. Towne, I like you very much. You're a terrific person and you've taught me so much about sewing that I never thought I'd have a chance to learn . . ."

"I've enjoyed it," said Mrs. Towne.

"I have too. And I appreciate your letting me help you out in exchange for lessons."

"But . . ." said Mrs. Towne. "There's a 'but,' isn't there?"

I nodded. "I love visiting. I like helping you. But I can't always come on the spur of the moment, like today. I have responsibilities in the Baby-sitters Club, and I'm teaching a kids' sewing class myself, and I have a family and friends . . . I mean, I need time for all that. And lately, it seems as if I haven't had any. As if I'm always answering a call from you."

I ducked my head. Then I thought, "Don't be a coward, Mary Anne." I looked up, wondering how angry and hurt Mrs. Towne would be.

She didn't seem angry at all. In fact, she was biting her lip, looking, well, embarrassed.

"Mrs. Towne? I'm sorry," I said.

"Don't be. Don't be one bit sorry, Mary Anne. You are absolutely right. I've been very selfish with you."

"No! You broke your ankle and it's been . . ."

Mrs. Towne raised her hand. "Hear me out. The last few times I've called, I haven't really needed your help. You know that and I know that. I just felt, well, lonely. I wanted some company. Not that I don't have friends of my own, my own age. But I liked your visits." She laughed. "It reminded me, I guess, of having my son around the house again somehow."

"Oh, Mrs. Towne."

"Mary Anne, can we still be friends, even though I've been so thoughtless and selfish?"

I couldn't believe it! Mrs. Towne thought she'd been selfish, and I thought I was the one being selfish.

"Don't say that! Of course we can still be friends. And we still have our sewing lessons . . ."

"Why don't we go back to our original arrangement for the lessons," suggested Mrs. Towne. "You can pay me with money instead of work."

I smiled gratefully. "I'd like that. But who will help you around here? You can't do everything yourself."

"No, I can't. But frankly, even before the accident, I was thinking of hiring a housekeeper to come in and help me. I've worked hard all my life. I deserve a little help now. So that's exactly what I'm going to do."

"It's a great idea," I said.

"Yes, it is," agreed Mrs. Towne. She hesitated, then said, "Would you like some tea?"

"I can't," I said. "I have to get home for dinner. But let's plan to visit regularly. Let's schedule a tea meeting right now."

"Great," said Mrs. Towne. "I'd like that."

"I would, too," I said. "Definitely."

As I rode my bicycle home, I felt very tired. Talking to Mrs. Towne had been hard. But I also felt sort of giddy and weightless. I hadn't realized how much of a chore visiting Mrs. Towne had become. If I had let things go on, in pursuit of some idea about being unselfish, I would have ended up hating those visits, I realized. And that would have been unfair to Mrs. Towne and to me.

Now I felt great. I'd kept Mrs. Towne as a friend, and I was looking forward to our next visit.

CHAPTER 14

"Y̲ou remember that junk food art show I had?" asked Claudia thoughtfully.

"Uh-huh," I answered, a little distractedly. It was the next to last quilting and sewing class and we were inside (our series of perfect summer days had been interrupted by rain) piecing together the squares of the quilt, which involved laying them out on the floor to see how they looked. With so many of the blocks appliquéd and embroidered and decorated with flowers, it was sort of like flower arranging. I shifted a red tulip on a blue background away from a pink rose on a darker pink background.

"I want a corner," said Vanessa.

"Okay," I replied. We'd laid out the quilt on paper long before, in one of the earliest classes. But that wasn't the same as seeing the finished blocks together.

"Well, what about a junk food quilt?"

"What, Claudia?"

Fortunately, she didn't seem to mind my distraction. She was, I realized, in the grip of creative vision. "A junk food quilt. You appliqué junk food designs on blocks, maybe even put stuffing under the appliqué to make the designs more three-dimensional, then join them together. It would be a statement about life, two basic needs joined in one presentation."

"What?" I said. "What are you talking about, Claud?"

"Food and warmth!" cried Claudia. "Can't you see it?"

"I don't think junk food counts as one of the basic needs in life," I answered.

"It does in *my* life," Claudia answered loftily, unfazed by my lack of enthusiasm.

"I like it," said Becca Ramsey.

"You do?" Claudia beamed.

"Yes, I love junk food. But my mother says junk food is bad for you."

"But do you like my idea?" asked Claudia.

Becca bent over and shifted one of her flower squares thoughtfully. "What idea?"

"Never mind," said Claudia. She caught my eye and said, "So I'll continue to be a great, unappreciated artist for awhile longer."

"Well, we appreciate you, Claud. So you're not a completely unappreciated artist."

"Thanks, Mary Anne. Underappreciated, then. I guess my public will have to wait." Claud squatted down by Charlotte Johanssen and said kindly, "Charlotte, I think you have your — tulip — upside down."

"No, I don't," said Charlotte. "It is growing that way."

"Oh. So it is," said Claudia. "I can see that now."

Just then, we heard a commotion at the front door: a series of thumps like someone running across the porch. But no one rang the door bell or knocked.

I opened the front door and looked outside. No one was there. Had I heard the wind? But the rain had stopped, at least for the moment, and there was no wind.

Another series of thuds, this time from near the back of the house, caught my attention. I closed the front door and locked it, then headed for the back. No one was there either.

Maybe it had been a gust of wind, I thought. I was glad it wasn't late at night, or I might have started worrying about ghosts — not that I believe in ghosts, of course.

Almost as soon as I returned to the den, we heard a muffled crash from outside.

"That does it," I said. I jumped up and headed for the back door.

"I'm coming, too," said Claudia.

"Me, too," said Claire.

"Why don't we all go?" said Claudia.

So the six of us went to the back door. No one was there. We trooped outside and I led the way around the side of the house — and spotted the shine of a yellow rain slicker in the shrubbery. I bent down and peered under the lower branches.

Nicky and Buddy were crouched there, looking half pleased, half scared.

"What are you guys doing?" I asked.

Sheepishly, they crawled out and stood up.

"Did we scare you?" asked Nicky.

"No," I said. "Were you trying to?"

Nicky and Buddy looked at each other and then back at me and shook their heads.

"No," said Nicky. "We just sort of came by to visit. See how things are going. You know."

Things? Could they possibly be curious about the quilt?

"Well, why didn't you knock on the door?" asked Claudia.

The boys shrugged.

"Hey, let's get out of the rain," I suggested.

"It's not raining," said Vanessa.

"Before it starts again," I said. "Come on in and take a look at the quilt. We're piecing it together now."

"I guess we could *look* at the quilt," said Buddy, and he and Nicky came inside with us. After the two boys had hung up their raincoats by the door, they followed us back to the den.

"We're laying the blocks out in the order we want, see?" said Claudia. "And then I'm going to draw a picture of the final design and we'll sew the blocks together according to the design."

"It looks okay," said Buddy.

"Thank you," I said.

"Has it been hard?" asked Nicky.

"I don't think so," I answered. "But then, we've all worked together."

"It's been fun," said Charlotte. "I want to make more quilts."

"Me, too," said Claire.

"Me three," said Vanessa.

"Me four," said Becca.

"Maybe we will," I said. "We've missed you guys. Maybe you'll join us if we make another quilt."

Nicky looked away. "I don't know," he told the far wall. "Maybe."

"I guess it is hard, though, if someone is teasing you about it," I went on.

Claudia had picked up her pencil, and was making a quick drawing of the design. "Sometimes I don't mind being teased," she said. "Sometimes my friends tease me, and it makes me laugh."

146

"I don't like being teased *ever*," Nicky declared to the wall.

"Me, neither," said Buddy.

"I guess it depends on who's doing the teasing. And why they're doing it. Maybe you could tell me who was teasing you guys."

"Clarence," said Nicky, suddenly looking right at me. "Clarence Morris."

"Oh," I said blankly.

"He's in our class at school. He lives a couple of blocks over," explained Buddy. "He's a real pain."

"A jerk," said Nicky.

"Yeah," Buddy agreed. "He teases everybody about everything. Like after I stopped sewing class? He started laughing at my bicycle." Buddy's outraged face told me what he thought of that.

"Yeah, and he teased me about having such a big family." Nicky looked, if possible, even more outraged. "I'd like to wreck him."

I said, "I don't think that would help, do you, Nicky?"

"Maybe. Maybe not. I'm not *going* to, anyway. I'm just going to ignore him."

"Does this mean," Claudia asked carefully, "that Clarence didn't *really* think it was weird and sissy for boys to sew?"

"He didn't care," said Nicky. "He just wanted to pick on us."

"Well, maybe you'd like to help us finish the quilt then," I suggested.

"That's okay," said Nicky quickly. He folded his arms, and threw out his chest, trying to look tough.

"Thanks," said Buddy. "But we'll just, you know, watch for awhile."

"Okay," I said.

"Ta-da!" Claudia held up the drawing. "Now, we'll divide the quilt into six sections, and each of us will take the squares for one section and sew them together according to this pattern."

After a little jockeying, we divided the chores up. By the time we were organized, Nicky and Buddy had sat down on the floor with us.

"Here," said Nicky. "I'll thread that needle for you. You want purple thread, right, Claudia?"

"Right. Thanks, Nicky."

A minute later, I head Buddy say to Vanessa, "Do you need a thimble? . . . Here."

You've probably guessed what happened next. Before long, Buddy and Nicky were as involved as everyone else with the quilt.

"Listen, you guys," I said to the boys, trying to sound casual. "Why don't I divide up my section and you two work on it. That way, I can help everybody out and sort of keep an eye on things."

"Well," said Nicky.

"You'd be helping me out," I said.

A few minutes later I looked over the bent heads of Buddy and Nicky as they helped finish the quilt. Claudia met my eyes and gave me a small, very discreet thumbs-up signal.

Nicky and Buddy were back. And I knew they'd show up for the last sewing class.

CHAPTER 15

The quilt was finished. Almost. It would have to be stretched on a frame and the front and backing quilted together, but the blocks had been sewn together. And each person had picked a favorite block and embroidered her or his name and date on it.

Buddy and Nicky had shown up for the last class — and they'd surprised me. They'd each made a block of their own: Nicky had finished his spider. And Buddy had made a cactus.

"They're beautiful," I said and I meant it.

"Will they fit in?" asked Buddy anxiously.

"Sure," I said. "We'll substitute your blocks for two of mine."

And that's what we did.

I could hardly wait for Mrs. Towne to see the quilt. Keeping it a secret during my sewing lessons with her was harder and harder. Of course, it helped that Mrs. Towne knew so many embroidery stitches and smocking techniques that it made my head spin. But I was learning them, gradually. And I was enjoying every minute of every class.

Finally the afternoon came when we'd decided to present Mrs. Towne with her quilt. We met at my house, where we packed the quilt carefully in a large box with lots of tissue paper. Then we carried it down Burnt Hill Road to Mrs. Towne's house.

I'd called Mrs. Towne earlier to ask her if I could stop by. She'd sounded pleased at the suggestion.

Buddy skipped up the steps ahead of us and rang the doorbell. A moment later, just as we'd lined up on the porch, Mrs. Towne opened the door.

"Well, what is all this?" she said.

"It's a surprise," answered Charlotte.

"Really? For me?"

"It sure is," I said.

"Come in, come in," said Mrs. Towne, stepping back.

I realized as I followed everyone through the door, that Mrs. Towne was walking without her cane.

I congratulated her. "Yes, isn't it wonderful? I'm so glad to get that cast off. My old ankle is as good as new, the doctor said."

"That's great, Mrs. Towne."

Since there were so many of us, Mrs. Towne

led us into her living room. "Won't you sit down?"

We all did, except me. I handed Mrs. Towne the box. "You inspired us," I said. "So we made this for you."

"It's a get-well present," Becca added. "And I guess it worked, because you've already gotten well!"

When Mrs. Towne lifted the quilt out of the box, she gasped. "It's just beautiful," she said. "Oh, it is so beautiful. You really made this for me?"

"Yes. It's a garden quilt. Because of your garden," Vanessa replied.

"And we each put our names on one of the blocks," said Becca. "See, there's mine."

"And mine," said Charlotte, jumping up. Of course everyone else jumped up, too, and soon Mrs. Towne was surrounded as each person pointed out his or her squares, and told stories about how they chose each flower and made each block.

At last Mrs. Towne laid the quilt carefully back in the box.

"I love it," she said. "I'll treasure it always and forever. It's the most beautiful quilt I've ever seen."

Vanessa wasn't fazed by the high praise Mrs. Towne had just given us. She nodded. "Thank you," she said.

We laughed then, and Mrs. Towne wiped her eyes. "What about some lemonade and cookies, everyone?" she asked.

Six voices, said, "Yes, please."

I said, "Mrs. Towne, could I have some tea?"

Mrs. Towne smiled at me. "You certainly can, Mary Anne. You stay right there. I'll fix everything and bring it out."

That night, after dinner, I took full advantage of the free time I suddenly had. Logan and I had made plans for the next day, I had a baby-sitting job lined up for Friday night — and in between I had nothing but free time to do anything — or nothing in.

"What are you smiling at?" Dawn asked, stopping in the open door of my room.

"Nothing," I said. "I'm smiling at a whole lot of nothing. Come on in."

A few minutes later we were still gossiping and hanging out. It felt great. And before long, I found myself confiding in Dawn about everything that had happened with Mrs. Towne.

"I didn't want to be selfish," I concluded. "I wanted to be less self-centered. But I was trying to please everyone else. And it was making me miserable."

Dawn nodded. "I don't think you're selfish or self-centered, Mary Anne. I think it is important to try to consider other people, but you have to consider yourself and your own needs, too. Otherwise, anything you do for anyone else, you can't do freely and unselfishly.

"You're right, Dawn," I replied gratefully. "That's exactly it."

Dawn nodded again, and then said slowly, "That's why I've been thinking about California lately. I miss my dad and Jeff and I can't ignore these feelings."

I sat straight up. "Oh, Dawn. I'm sorry!"

"Thanks," Dawn answered softly. "You know, having someone who understands helps. Talking helps, too. I'm glad I've figured out I don't just have to be miserable and miss my father. I can do something about those feelings."

Somewhere inside, I'd known Dawn was missing her father and brother a lot. I'd just tried to pretend that all her references to California were casual.

But I'd sensed they weren't, even if I hadn't wanted to admit it.

That *had* been selfish. And self-centered.

So I took a deep breath. "I'm really, really sorry I didn't listen sooner, Dawn. But I'm here now and I *do* understand."

"Do you?" said Dawn, looking at me.

I felt tears welling in my eyes, but I gave her a watery smile. "I do."

"Oh, Mary Anne," wailed Dawn.

"Oh, Dawn," I said, the tears beginning to slide down my cheeks.

And then I gave my sister and my best friend a big, long hug.

"It'll be okay," I said. "Whatever happens, it'll be okay."

And I knew it would.

About the Author

ANN M. MARTIN did *a lot* of baby-sitting when she was growing up in Princeton, New Jersey. Now her favorite baby-sitting charge is her cat, Mouse, who lives with her in her Manhattan apartment.

Ann Martin's Apple Paperbacks include *Yours Turly, Shirley; Ten Kids, No Pets; With You and Without You; Bummer Summer;* and all the other books in the Baby-sitters Club series.

She is a former editor of books for children, and was graduated from Smith College. She likes ice cream, the beach, and *I Love Lucy;* and she hates to cook.

Look for #67

DAWN'S BIG MOVE

Mom and Mary Anne laughed. They both looked happy. Richard looked happy, too.

Me? I was sort of staring at the grass. I *wasn't* feeling happy. I should have been. It was a gorgeous day, warm and summery. We were having a great time. But something was wrong.

My California homesickness was getting worse by the day. And it made me feel sooo guilty. I mean, I love my life in Stoneybrook. I had my mom and my friends. Richard was always sweet to me. Mary Anne was the best sister I could imagine having.

I didn't want to say anything. Everyone was having a fabulous time that day, and it wouldn't be right to burst the bubble.

"Dawn?" Mary Anne said gently. "What's wrong?"

"I want to go home!" The words just stumbled right out of my mouth. I couldn't hold them back.

Fsssssht! The bubble was burst. Richard's smile faded, and he glanced at Mom. Mary Anne shifted herself to be next to me.

I just hung my head lower and played with a few strands of grass.

"You've been thinking about them so much lately," Mary Anne said.

I nodded. I could barely get the word "Yes" to come out.

Mom sighed. "Well, I suppose I should call Dad and figure out a good weekend. It'll be hard to get tickets, you know — "

"I don't mean *go back*, like, go back for a weekend," I interrupted. "I mean really go back. To stay. Like for a few months."

"A few months?" Mom looked shocked.

Even I was surprised at what I'd said. But it was true. I just hadn't wanted to admit it. Not even to myself.

**Read all the latest books
in the Baby-sitters Club series
by Ann M. Martin**

#40 *Claudia and the Middle School Mystery*
Can the Baby-sitters find out who the cheater is at
SMS?

#41 *Mary Anne vs. Logan*
Mary Anne thought she and Logan would be together forever. . . .

#42 *Jessi and the Dance School Phantom*
Someone — or some*thing* — wants Jessi out of the
show.

#43 *Stacey's Emergency*
The Baby-sitters are so worried. Something's
wrong with Stacey.

#44 *Dawn and the Big Sleepover*
One hundred kids, thirty pizzas — it's Dawn's
biggest baby-sitting job ever!

#45 *Kristy and the Baby Parade*
Will the Baby-sitters' float take first prize in the
Stoneybrook Baby Parade?

#46 *Mary Anne Misses Logan*
But does Logan miss *her*?

#47 *Mallory on Strike*
Mallory needs a break from baby-sitting — even if
it means quitting the club.

#48 *Jessi's Wish*
Jessi makes a very special wish for a little girl with
cancer.

161

Mysteries:

7 *Dawn and the Disappearing Dogs*
Someone's been stealing dogs all over Stoney-brook!

8 *Jessi and the Jewel Thieves*
Jessi and her friend Quint are busy tailing two jewel thieves from the Big Apple!

9 *Kristy and the Haunted Mansion*
Kristy and the Krashers are spending the night in a spooky old house!

#10 *Stacey and the Mystery Money*
Who would give Stacey counterfeit money?

#11 *Claudia and the Mystery at the Museum*
Burglaries, forgeries . . . something crooked is going on at the new museum in Stoneybrook!

Special Editions (Readers' Request):

Logan's Story
Being a boy baby-sitter isn't easy!

Logan Bruno, Boy Baby-sitter
Has Logan decided he's too cool for baby-sitting?

THE BABY-SITTERS CLUB®

by Ann M. Martin

More titles... ❯

❑ MG44970-2 #49 Claudia and the Genius of Elm Street	$3.25
❑ MG44969-9 #50 Dawn's Big Date	$3.25
❑ MG44968-0 #51 Stacey's Ex-Best Friend	$3.25
❑ MG44966-4 #52 Mary Anne + 2 Many Babies	$3.25
❑ MG44967-2 #53 Kristy for President	$3.25
❑ MG44965-6 #54 Mallory and the Dream Horse	$3.25
❑ MG44964-8 #55 Jessi's Gold Medal	$3.25
❑ MG45657-1 #56 Keep Out, Claudia!	$3.25
❑ MG45658-X #57 Dawn Saves the Planet	$3.25
❑ MG45659-8 #58 Stacey's Choice	$3.25
❑ MG45660-1 #59 Mallory Hates Boys (and Gym)	$3.25
❑ MG45662-8 #60 Mary Anne's Makeover	$3.50
❑ MG45663-6 #61 Jessi's and the Awful Secret	$3.50
❑ MG45664-4 #62 Kristy and the Worst Kid Ever	$3.50
❑ MG45665-2 #63 Claudia's Friend Friend	$3.50
❑ MG45666-0 #64 Dawn's Family Feud	$3.50
❑ MG45667-9 #65 Stacey's Big Crush	$3.50
❑ MG45575-3 Logan's Story Special Edition Readers' Request	$3.25
❑ MG44240-6 Baby-sitters on Board! Super Special #1	$3.95
❑ MG44239-2 Baby-sitters' Summer Vacation Super Special #2	$3.95
❑ MG43973-1 Baby-sitters' Winter Vacation Super Special #3	$3.95
❑ MG42493-9 Baby-sitters' Island Adventure Super Special #4	$3.95
❑ MG43575-2 California Girls! Super Special #5	$3.95
❑ MG43576-0 New York, New York! Super Special #6	$3.95
❑ MG44963-X Snowbound Super Special #7	$3.95
❑ MG44962-X Baby-sitters at Shadow Lake Super Special #8	$3.95
❑ MG45661-X Starring the Baby-sitters Club Super Special #9	$3.95

Available wherever you buy books...or use this order form.

Scholastic Inc., P.O. Box 7502, 2931 E. McCarty Street, Jefferson City, MO 65102

Please send me the books I have checked above. I am enclosing $————
(please add $2.00 to cover shipping and handling). Send check or money order - no cash or C.O.D.s please.

Name ———————————————————————————————

Address ————————————————————————————————

City————————————————— State/Zip —————————————
Please allow four to six weeks for delivery. Offer good in the U.S. only. Sorry, mail orders are not available to residents of Canada. Prices subject to change.

BSC1292

Don't miss out on
The All New

B·A·B·Y-S·I·T·T·E·R·S®

Fan Club

Join now!
Your one-year membership package includes:

- The exclusive Fan Club T-Shirt!
- A Baby-sitters Club poster!
- A Baby-sitters Club note pad and pencil!
- An official membership card!
- The exclusive *Guide to Stoneybrook!*

Plus four additional newsletters per year

so you can be the first to know the hot news about the series — Super Specials, Mysteries, Videos, and more — the baby-sitters, Ann Martin, and lots of baby-sitting fun from the Baby-sitters Club Headquarters!

ALL THIS FOR JUST $6.95 plus $1.00 postage and handling! **You can't get all this great stuff anywhere else except THE BABY-SITTERS FAN CLUB!**

Just fill in the coupon below and mail with payment to: THE BABY-SITTERS FAN CLUB, Scholastic Inc., P.O. Box 7500, 2931 E. McCarty Street, Jefferson City, MO 65102.

THE BABY-SITTERS FAN CLUB

___ YES! Enroll me in The Baby-sitters Fan Club! I've enclosed my check or money order (no cash please) for $7.95

Name _____ Birthdate _____

Street _____

City _____ State/Zip _____

Where did you buy this book?

❑ Bookstore   ❑ Drugstore   ❑ Supermarket
❑ Book Fair   ❑ Book Club   ❑ other_____

BSFC593

How would YOU like to visit Universal Studios in Orlando, Florida?

Check out the sights!

Experience the rides!

Tour the Studios!

Enter

Summer Super Special Giveaway for your chance to win!

We'll send one grand prize winner and a parent or guardian on an all expense paid trip to Universal Studios in Orlando, Florida for 3 days and 2 nights!

25 second prize winners receive a Baby-sitters Club Fun Pack filled with a Baby-sitters Club T-Shirt, "Songs For My Best Friends" cassette, Baby-sitters Club stationery and more!

All you have to do is fill out the coupon below or write the information on a 3" x 5" piece of paper and mail to:

THE BABY-SITTERS CLUB SUMMER SUPER SPECIAL GIVEAWAY P.O. Box 7500, Jefferson City, MO 65102. Return by November 30 1993.

- -

THE SUMMER SUPER SPECIAL GIVEAWAY

Name_____ Birthdate _____

Address _____

City_____State/Zip _____

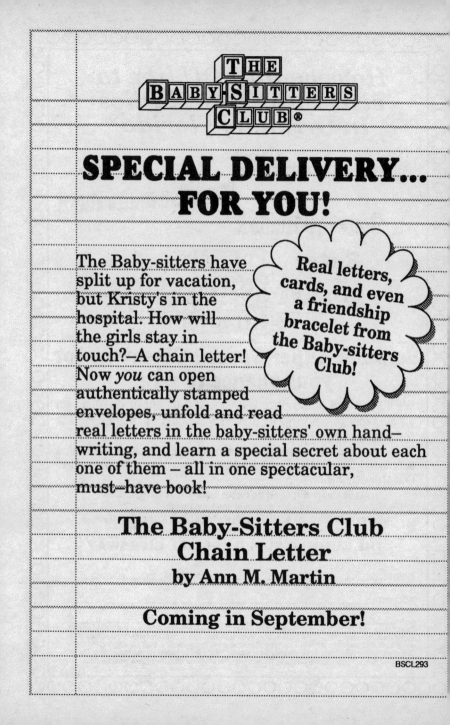